*Enjoy the read*
*Happy Xmas.*

# *Chester* *...*

# The Scouse Mouse with No Nous

## Thomas J Sweeney

**Email: bandttsweeney@gmail.com**
**Word count: 31,924**

Life has not been easy for Chester the Mouse,

He was born under rotten floorboards in an old Liverpool house.

He wasn't the cleverest, the smartest of mice,

When you could tell another mouse once you had to tell Chester twice.

His brothers and sisters were quick-witted and mature,

Chester was the opposite, so silly and unsure.

He laughed and he joked and played hundreds of tricks,

Which landed him in trouble and many a fix.

His mum Maisie encouraged but would often despair,

As he ignored all the wisdom she had chosen to share.

Things had to change and change very fast,

For Chester's foolhardiness simply could not last.

And then, as predicted, a terrible event,

Brought Chester heartbreak and lots of torment.

A rash decision that was very confusing,

Led to a journey not of his choosing.

Dangers a-plenty, adventures galore,

Caused Chester to show qualities he'd never shown before.

It was now that he needed a strength from within,

Did he find it? Well, read on,

For now is the time for his story to begin.

# Table of Contents

# 1 The Loving Family

The moon was making its escape, going back to wherever it had come from, taking with it the long shadows that had enveloped the Liverpool football stadium throughout the night. The new morn now began its entrance as the dim light started to replace the stubborn darkness. All was peaceful except for the occasional whistle from the early bird, as the dawn chorus was soon to begin. The distant sounds of clinking bottles could also be heard as a weary milkman hastily assembled his orders.

The Anfield district of Liverpool was quiet for now, but in a few short hours the silence would be no more as the streets would become invaded by a hustling and bustling, pushing and shoving mass of people making their way to many a destination, in a seemingly disorganised way. Cars, lorries and buses would add to the chaos, as children, bound for school, excitedly skipped alongside mothers. But all that was to come later, as for now, in the backyards that ran the length of the cobbled alleyways, under damp cardboard, old rusty bike frames, car tyres and rubble, another world began to stir.

After a hectic night followed by a few hours of inactivity, once again mice would use the virgin daylight to their advantage, and forage for more opportunities to feed as the alley cats retired back through their flaps.

In a large Victorian terraced house in St. Domingo Vale, under the creaking and splintered floorboards, tiny feet could be heard scurrying about as Maisie the mouse paced up and down as her latest brood of pups hastily assembled in the cramped space below the disused toilet. It was not the ideal place to hold what was to be a very important meeting, but lots of other mouse mothers who were about to deliver a similar talk to their children had commandeered the best spots under the bedrooms, the attic and the living room. For today was the day Maisie, successful mother of seventy-six previous children, would say her final farewell to the fifteen starry-eyed offspring she had given birth to only three and a half weeks earlier. She would lecture them, warning of the dangers of the outside world – and there were many. She would tell of the opportunities to be had as they embarked on their new life and left the safety of the nest. A nest that they would have to vacate, as a heavily pregnant Maisie would soon need it again. She would tell of the need to be vigilant at all times, for the unwary could meet with an unfortunate end.

The alley cats were cunning and very stealthy, stalking silently before the pounce: there would be no escape. "The rats are not to be trusted and it has to be said, they will kill and eat you once the hunt is done. We look the same, we act the same, but beware, because we are not the same," she would say.

She would know at this point in her address that her gathered clan would have expressions of horror etched on their open-mouthed little faces, but she would continue.

"The real danger though, the real enemy you will face, are the humans. They will entice you with little tit-bits of food, they will call out encouraging you to show yourself whilst armed with all manner of things, ready to deliver the fatal blow. They will set traps smeared with the most delicious of our favourite foods, but a food very few will get to taste." Maisie stopped her pacing up and down and turned to face the attentive congregation. Her big brown eyes moistened as she cleared her throat. It would soon be time to begin her well-rehearsed speech.

"Are we all here?" she asked inquisitively as she began a count of all the heads.

Everybody looked around, checking along with her, and a few seconds later Tocky, the smallest mouse in the group, replied, "Yes, mum!" in a very excited voice whilst, wondering what was about to happen.

Tocky liked to be first in everything he did, he showed imagination, a will to succeed, all the traits mice needed to stand them in good stead for the future. Mum Maisie thanked him and concluded the count. She thought to herself that this was a very good brood; she had very few worries about this litter. Maisie knew every one of her pups by sight and by name. She would remember them for a long time after they had left the nest because, periodically, she would bump into them again. She had long stopped using such names as Albert and Angel, Ben and Bubbles, Charlie and Cherry, because having had so many babies, she found it difficult to keep coming up with new ones. In fact, she found herself almost repeating some. She had now started naming her children after all the districts of Liverpool, such as Tocky for Toxteth, Crocky for Croxteth, Norris for Norris Green and so on and so forth. She found it was a lot easier to do this.

Maisie began. "Anfield, children, is a much-changed place," she announced, her voice dominant with a firm tone. "A few years ago, these alleyways that crisscross our territory, providing us with safety, our food, our very existence, were rubbish-strewn with all manner of things discarded by the humans. Food was in abundance and there were many places for us to live and to hide; it was a joyous time, a time of plenty, but also because of the rich pickings it became a more dangerous place for us to live. You may ask why that would be so." She paused to gauge the reaction, then continued "Because, Children, we became fat and lazy, forgetting all our instincts and impulses that have been learned over many centuries and passed down by our ancestors, therefore creating more situations for us to fall foul of our many enemies." Pausing once more, she walked silently amongst her family, who were all now concentrating on her every word. She took a deep breath and sighed, "Well, things have changed and for whatever reason," she said in a more whispered tone, "the humans have stopped throwing out their rubbish; they have cleared away the mess they had created, and put gates at all the entrances of the alleyways to stop other humans leaving their waste. They scrub and they brush with soapy suds leaving numerous odours, odours I shouldn't but I do admit to liking. Times have become much leaner for us and we have had to adapt, and forage further and further a-field. There are, however, some humans who continue their old ways and make a real mess in their yards, and for this we have to be thankful. You will experience hunger," and with her voice now faltering she added, "and some of you will not make it through." She momentarily paused once again as she gathered her composure; it was as she had thought – there was now a look of anxiety and disbelief all around. Their innocence was destroyed by her hard-hitting talk. "Welcome to the real world," she mused. Oh, how she hated saying such things, but the message had to get through. "Life as a mouse can be very hard and only the most alert and wary will survive." Maisie continued and told of the cats and the rats and the ways of the humans.

She thought she had covered every eventuality and came to the point when she felt it was the appropriate time to lighten the mood and talk of the many opportunities and also the good times that lay ahead.

"For those of you who have listened and heeded what I have said, you will become strong and live through to the time of the year when life becomes so much better for us all," she explained with a happier expression, and a radiant smile appeared on her face. "We are lucky that we live where we do; Anfield is a unique place as, at certain times of the year, the humans arrive in full force. At first, they announce their presence with the distant patter of footsteps, this builds as they get closer and closer and before long there is a great thunder of noise. Like an army marching, they arrive and enter the stadium, and shout and scream at the tops of their voices, worshipping whatever it is they worship, and a few hours later the thunderous paces return and then disintegrate and disappear back to where they came from. This event seems to happen quite often, and in their wake the humans leave behind all manner of edible goodies," she excitedly announced. "There are pastries and crisps, fish in batter, chips and sugary sweets. We can gorge ourselves and we do, and when we can gorge no more, our stores become bloated and see us through until the crowds return. "'Oh, I am making myself hungry just thinking about it," she declared loudly, as the children all laughed together, pleading with their mum to tell them some more. "Well," she said, warming to the task, as she now had her brood on side, "Sometimes, after many months of the screaming and the shouting, the crowds gather again, but this time there seem to be many more of them – thousands and thousands in fact. Cars cannot be seen, but a lone bus always appears and the humans at the top of it hold aloft a silvery thing, and sometimes they have two silvery things. "Well," she continued, "when they do this everybody goes wild and cheers; it's quite deafening; it goes on for ages, and as the bus snakes its way up Oakfield Road, the humans follow it. Later on, as quiet descends once again, everything seems eerily peaceful and tranquil; then it is *our* time. Food is everywhere We collect as much as we can and then go back for more. There is so much you cannot believe your eyes, so much that, in fact, a lot of it will be wasted. It's at these times that we will often invite all of our mouse friends over from Everton to join us in the banquet, as there is plenty for everyone. And I have got to say this, every now and again, and it is only now and again, the same thing happens over there at Goodison Park, Everton, and they show off a silvery thing and we are all invited to their feast."

Tocky chuckled loudly at this, as did Norris and the rest of the siblings, and some hysterically fell from their perches. The gloomy atmosphere that had descended was now quickly displaced by a feeling of genuine expectancy, a looking forward attitude, and with this Crocky yelled out loudly, *"Three cheers for Mum!"*

Everybody joined in with a resounding *"Hip hip hooray! Hip hip hooray! Hip hip hooray!"* and then they all stood up, but before they could cheer, another chant of "Hooray" rang out, stopping everyone in their tracks.

"Who or what was that?" asked a surprised Maisie.

"I don't know," Tocky replied nervously, "but it seemed to come from behind that brick in the corner."

Maisie gestured to her children to be quiet as she crept up towards the identified stone, showing a bravery only a mother can show. Ever so slowly she began to peer around the heavy obstacle to find the cause for her concern, when suddenly a loud *"COOEE!"* broke the silence and a small furry brown ball jumped out. The startled Maisie screamed in horror as she instinctively leapt two feet backwards, slightly hitting her head on the flooring above, before landing softly in a heap of fine dust that had settled over a hundred years. An explosion of minute particles filled the air as Maisie disappeared from view. The trembling and now huddled together Children, all breathed a sigh of relief and collectively shouted out,

"IT'S CHESTER!" as they started rolling about with laughter and even more laughter as their now blackened mother re-appeared out of the haze. Coughing and spluttering, Maisie brushed herself down and had a good shake, sending even more dust clouds airborne. She scowled angrily at her children. The laughter immediately stopped, but she saved her biggest scowl for Chester.

"Don't move, don't you *dare* move; I will deal with you later," Maisie threatened. Chester froze. Maisie made her way back to her original spot, still trying to free herself of her powdery covering, but the cobwebs were proving particularly sticky.

Maisie stood silently and gazed at her brood; they then all rushed forward and began hugging and touching as they quickly surrounded her. Tears flowed as it was now time to go, time for them to leave, to make their own way in a world their mother had described, a world they had visited before with their protector but never alone.

Maisie reluctantly freed herself from the strong embraces, "Goodbye Tocky," she spluttered, "Look after yourself, won't you? Goodbye, Norris. Take care, Walton, Crocky, Knotty, Mossley. Safe journey, Orrell, Faz, Dingle, Gatty, Dove, Belle. Be careful. Edge, Club, chins up," she continued and finally, "Gil, my little Gil." Maisie took her into her arms and squeezed tightly. Little Gil let out a slight moan. Maisie kissed her head, turned on her heels and crossed to the other side of the room. Her eyes were now swimming with tears as she bade them farewell.

Tocky was first to show initiative as he led the way out from underneath the toilet, and precariously negotiated the steep, bare stairs. He was quickly followed by his fourteen brothers and sisters, and soon they all arrived at the broken air brick, a well-used entrance and exit. A mass prolonged hug ensued with lots of kisses, a last glance around and, as quickly as they had gathered, they were gone, for mice cannot afford to idle.

Maisie dabbed her eyes and collected her thoughts and quickly returned to the task in hand. She strode purposefully towards where Chester had been told to stay and for once he had obeyed her, but if there had been any softening, any mellowing in her planned approach to dealing with him, it quickly disappeared for Chester stood there statuesquely as if frozen. His left front paw was raised high off the ground and his right rear leg twitched slightly as he held it aloft.

*"What are you doing Chester!"* Maisie shrieked, "Put your feet down." She couldn't help it. "You're such a fool," she added without thinking.

Chester put down his legs and quickly regained his balance, "But you told me not to move so I didn't," he declared triumphantly and a smile creased his face, as he thought he had got one over on his mum.

Chester was a very small mouse, born to Maisie almost four months previously. Three more litters of pups had been given birth to since and had felt the love of Maisie, had done all of the preparatory work, and had gone. But not Chester; he was still hanging around the nest, either too fearful to strike out on his own and make his way in life, or just incapable of doing this. The latter was closer to the truth. Chester was locked into his immature world; he had hardly any of the instincts he should have had and should have had a long, long time ago. He thought everything was a joke, and a laugh. But this attitude and his ways could and almost had got him into serious trouble before. Maisie despaired of Chester; she had long run out of patience with him. She did not have the time or the inclination anymore to spend teaching him and pointing him in the right direction.

"Chester, Chester, Chester, what am I going to do with you?" Maisie muttered. There was a slightly defeatist resignation in her voice as she shook her head repeatedly whilst burying it in her hands. "Have you not learned anything these past months? Have you not taken in what I have said to try and help you to succeed? What is your problem, because I really cannot take much more of this? You are starting to test my resolve. Grow up, will you, grow up," she pleaded in desperation, her anger building. She continued the verbal assault for she was now at the end of her tether. The rage that had been bubbling just beneath the surface erupted and Maisie shouted out once again, *"WHAT IS YOUR PROBLEM?!"*

Chester recoiled in horror; he had never seen his mother like this before, and as he began to tremble ever so slightly, he thought better of saying something funny. Chester now stood bolt upright and faced his mum. He summoned his courage and after a little thought began his reply, "It's... it's..." Chester stuttered, struggling to finish his sentence or to even make a start. "It's because...," Chester hesitated once more. Maisie interrupted and in an encouraging voice, prompted Chester to continue,

"It's because of what, Chester, because of what?" Chester sensed her softening tone and as a feeling of relaxation swept over his stiffening body, he now began to feel more comfortable, ready to voice whatever explanation he had.

"I feel so confused, mum, so confused," Chester quietly whispered as he choked back some tears. Maisie moved closer placing her arm around her son's shoulders, imploring him to continue. Regaining his composure Chester, blurted out,

"Well, it's because I don't know what I am mum. You tell me that I am a mouse but I am not so sure, it's all so confusing for me as all my other thoughts become muddled and I have great difficulty thinking straight, and so I tend to act very silly." Maisie, taken aback by Chester's outburst, tried unsuccessfully to suppress a smile; she hadn't really expected to hear what she had just heard.

"What on earth do you mean, Chester?" Maisie enquired, "You don't know whether you are a mouse? Please explain."

"You won't laugh will you, Mum. I feel so embarrassed, but I do need to talk," Chester asked, whilst looking for reassurance. Maisie promised not to laugh and gave him the reassurance he required, telling him she was there to help. Chester, now feeling more comfortable with the situation, began his bizarre explanation with a confidence that had been missing before. "Well, it's the humans, isn't it? I sneak into Mrs. Jones's yard at number twenty-four and she calls out to me, "Hello little Mousey, and how are you today little Mousey?" whilst throwing bits of fruit cake and biscuits to me. I eat them very quickly and they are really scrummy. This has been going on for quite some time. And then at other times I go into that woman's yard at number thirty-six, the woman with the huge shock of white hair with the long streak of black down the centre. She chases after me, broom in hand raised high above her head, and as she tries to hit me with it, she shrieks at the top of her voice, *Get out of here you little so-and-so!* And all manner of other unrepeatable things." Maisie kept her promise and didn't laugh. She listened some more as Chester continued to unburden himself. "And then the humans put out food for us, lots of it, and then they go and wrap it up and hide it in a big black bag, and sometimes two black bags – I don't understand that at all. We then have to wait until the cats rip them open and then watch as they claim all the best bits for themselves." Chester looked at his Mum in total bewilderment waiting for her reply. Maisie raised her paw to her mouth. "You are not going to laugh are you, Mum? You said you wouldn't," the agitated Chester reminded her.

"No, no, no," Maisie quickly responded, "I had…
err… some dust in my throat." She let out a weak cough
but it wasn't the truth. Maisie, feeling the need to change
the subject, implored Chester to carry on. Chester believed
his Mum and resumed his outpourings.

"And what about the time the humans put out all
that blue food in little trays for us? I didn't like it very
much; it made my tummy very sore." Maisie suddenly
became more alert and angrily interrupted Chester as she
remembered that terrible episode,

"YES, and you brought some of it home to feed to
my babies. It was only with luck that I was there to stop
you."

Chester, feeling rather foolish, meekly responded in
his defence, "Well, I didn't know it was poisoned bait."

Maisie was now angry again. It was an anger born
more out of her frustration with Chester's lack of wisdom
and his total naivety. It was her turn now as she went on the

attack, "And what about the time the humans, whilst searching for our entrances and exits, placed little containers of red liquid everywhere. Every mouse walked past them but not you. Straight through them, red footprints led straight to our door and the enemy sealed us in. It was only because we had lots of mother's milk that our babies survived." The irate Maisie continued her rant: "It took four days and thirty-six mice to nibble through that air brick and free us all."

Chester smiled to himself and then declared sheepishly, "Okay, I'll give you that one, Mum," and they both burst out laughing together as the memory came flooding back. Maisie's laughing slowed and then stopped as she caught sight of a look in Chester that was all too familiar. Chester was beginning to look more and more like his father, Handsome Ted.

Ahh! Handsome Ted, she mused, allowing her thoughts to wander momentarily, and then as the heavily pregnant Maisie looked down at her ever-expanding waistline, her senses quickly returned and she growled, "Wait till I see that Handsome Ted."

Maisie and Chester hugged each other tightly, and that hug triggered a flow of tears from the two of them; there was definitely a strong bond between mother and son. In the ensuing minutes, Maisie once again told Chester where she thought he was going wrong. He listened intently to his mother before saying he now understood better and promising he would try much harder and make her very proud of him.

"Thank you so much, Mum. I really did need that talk," he started to say as a whistle pierced the air, interrupting him.

"Who is that?" asked the surprised Maisie. Chester quickly supplied the answer,

"Oh, that will be Giblet. He said he would be calling for me today," and with that Chester turned to leave, and then quickly turned back once more to face his Mum. He didn't speak; his smile said it all, and then he was off. Little did Maisie know that the day Chester would leave would come a lot sooner than she thought.

## 2   A Friend in Need... Can be a Burden

Maisie was glad Giblet was very close to Chester. She felt happy and more relaxed when they were together as Giblet was really sensible and would look out for Chester and steer him away from any trouble. Giblet and Chester were about the same age and were both very small in size; maybe this was the reason they had become such firm friends.

"Hello, Giblet. You're late. I thought you would be here sooner!" Chester said loudly, as he greeted his pal.

"I have had to be really watchful this morning as it's bin bag day. Everyone is putting them out in their yards and alleyways, and there seem to be more than ever. That has slowed me down," Giblet quietly responded. "Normally it only takes me around five minutes to reach your house, but the bags have brought out the cats and the rats early, and I can smell them everywhere as they search for their fill. Careful today, Chester, be *very* careful. Are you listening to me?" Giblet demanded. Chester nodded, saying that he understood, but then he quite often nodded saying that he understood.

Both mice made their way down the bare stairs and arrived at the broken air brick, then together they cautiously put their heads through and smelt the cool morning air. A slight drizzle had started to descend, Giblet knew this would make their task doubly difficult as the falling rain would mask out all the sounds of any approaching dangers and wash away the rogue odours. Giblet looked to his left, Chester looked to his right. Giblet looked to his right and Chester looked to his left, and without another word being said, both managed to squeeze through the small opening together. The wet cobbles with their differing sizes made walking very difficult, but Giblet with all of his experience negotiated the well-used trail like an expert. He sidled up as close as possible to the red brick walls; these covered his left flank – one less problem in case of attack. Giblet turned to check Chester's progress, and to his dismay, and to no real surprise, caught sight of Chester going in the opposite direction.

"Chester, oh Chester, over here if you don't mind." Giblet's voice with a sarcastic tone exploded into Chester's big ears.

"Sorry, Giblet," Chester stammered as he quickly readjusted his position and fell into line behind his pal. They now began to move together. There could be no more delays as the morning was getting on. Giblet crossed quickly from one side of the sodden alley to the next, furiously sniffing the gaps under each back-yard door, trying to get the faintest whiff or tell-tale smell of the bounty he was searching for. Chester could detect all manner of delicious things at every door; his nose was twitching and his head was held high as he tasted the air.

"Why not this yard?" Chester moaned. "Why not this yard?" Chester nagged. "This one?" Chester pleaded. Chester griped, Chester groaned, Chester whinged on.

Giblet was not named Giblet for nothing; oh no, he knew what he was looking for. The reason for his reluctance not to enter just any old site was that he loved chicken, succulent chicken. He couldn't get enough of it; he loved the fibrous flesh, the crispy chewy-skin, the savoury moisture. The thought of it drove him on as he bypassed yet another yard. Chester remained puzzled but he reluctantly followed. Five minutes later, two more passages, eighteen more doors passed, two maybes and two might-bes, Giblet suddenly pulled up sharply. Chester clumsily head-butted Giblet's bum, bringing him to an abrupt halt.

"Is this the place? Is this the one?" Chester enquired excitedly as he regained his senses. "Is it?" he continued. There was no answer. Giblet's nose was now doing the talking, twitching furiously as creases etched his tiny face and his whiskers vibrated rapidly. Giblet's big ears were talking also, telling him there was danger here, BIG danger. They must not rush in. Giblet's look calmed the eager Chester.

The old grey door that loomed large before them had long since fallen from its rusty hinges; there were no gaps to peer under here. Splits and splinters covered the weather-ravaged twisted barrier that looked a thousand feet high to a small mouse. Holes that once housed a strong knot now mottled the weak wood, and the flaked paint that was once a protection now fell like snow at the slightest touch. Giblet craned his neck and peered skywards; he could just about make out the number eighty-six; he would remember this for future visits, because he planned more, for the strong smells of what he desired most were, without a doubt, behind that door. Giblet took several deep breaths and a few smaller ones, trying to summon up the courage to overcome his nervousness as he surveyed the problem before him. He didn't survey for long because mice are equipped for most challenges, and Giblet was no different.

"Stay here, Chester, I will be back soon. *Don't move!*" Giblet ordered, and Chester unconvincingly agreed. Giblet had a good shake and expelled a fine spray of water this way and that, and also towards Chester, who saw it coming, but remembering Giblet had told him not to move, he didn't. His eyes were soon wet, but it wasn't from tears.

Rearing up onto his hind legs, Giblet rubbed his hands together; they were soon dry. He reached upwards and easily gained a good grip; his back feet shuffled against the bare wood, and with lightning speed, Giblet targeted a gaping hole and effortlessly raced up. Giblet could not believe his eyes as he popped his head through the large cavity. Row upon row of bin bags, stacked unevenly, reached for the sky. There had obviously been a party here last night, he thought to himself. Slash marks had helped release some of their cargo as all manner of things flowed out. The cats had done their job well, but to Giblet's dismay they were still there.

Giblet had smelt her and Giblet had heard her a few moments earlier, and now he could see her. He didn't need to see the face that rummaged deep inside the shiny black plastic; the long sleek muscular tiger-striped body told it all, for this was not just any old flea-ridden, broken-toothed alley cat, no, this was *Tarla*, super-sized, super agile, vicious to the core. This was her territory, fought for and captured in many bloody encounters long ago. Other cats now kept their distance or surrendered meekly in her presence, as her loud yowls that screamed out through the night told them that she was still Top Cat: Top Cat, top mother, and mouse killer. She had seen it all, done it all, and had probably eaten it all.

Giblet's concentration was total and his balance perfect; he dare not move in the slightest as his life surely depended on it. His steely stare was now fixed on Tarla, and also her kitten, Evil, who had just slunk into view. He had his mother's looks and her ways; he was definitely Tarla's son. Evil purred gleefully as he lapped quickly at a newly-found splodge of gateau, unaware of the audience above. Tarla stopped her rummaging and reversed out from inside the larder she had found, to reveal herself fully. A chicken drumstick was clasped firmly in her teeth, and a few scars adorned her face. They were the only reminders of past wars.

Chester now moved. "What's happening? What can you see, Giblet?" he called out in a voice neither quiet nor loud. Giblet did not need to hear this at this time and whilst his front end remained stiff and unmoved, his back leg waved furiously down towards Chester trying to shush him and tell him to be quiet. Well, that didn't work, did it? For this was Chester wasn't it? Chester stepped backwards and made a run and a jump towards the slippery door, and promptly fell back to earth as he failed miserably to gain a foothold. Undaunted, Chester brushed himself down and after three more noisy attempts, succeeded in his quest to join his pal high up above. He had also succeeded in alerting Tarla, who had now stopped her feasting; her large eyes were now fixed in that direction. The exhausted Chester paused momentarily as he gulped the air. His exertions had taken their toll and without further ado he forced his head through the tiniest of openings and announced loudly to Giblet, "What's happening?" He had now definitely also announced his presence to Tarla.

Tarla's eyes pierced the morning gloom and the slowing rain as they immediately homed in on their target; her sensitive ears had not let her down. Two pathetic brown furry heads with bulging eyes lost in a sea of broken wood now came into view. Tarla knew those shapes well and instinctively crouched low. Her legs disappeared beneath her proud chest, her stare was unwavering. Evil had adopted the same pose, for he had been taught well, and now the hunt was on.

One mouse head moved as one mouse head remained still. Giblet could be relied upon in these situations; rain ran into his eyes but he did not blink. Chester shook his head from side to side, blinked incessantly, breathed heavily, snorted, sniffed, readjusted his position, but apart from that he was really quiet. Giblet, through gritted teeth, told Chester to "Shut up, shut up, please." He hoped his message would be heard, and heard quickly. Chester now recognised his rigid friend's look, even though Giblet continued to look straight ahead.

The seriousness of their plight now hit home as both mice detected Evil's paws moving, one after the other in a forward motion; his stealthy body duly followed. There was now no way they could escape. Both mice began to tremble, fearing the end could be near. But then, miraculously, Tarla hissed loudly, stopping Evil in his tracks, telling him not to waste his energy, for they were both well fed. Evil looked up menacingly towards Chester and Giblet with a look that said, "You will do for another day." Giblet and Chester, who were now too scared to move in case they reignited the cats' interest, remained suspended high up on their lofty perches, and as Evil returned to his cake, Giblet sighed a sigh of relief. Chester didn't sigh though, he just hoped Evil would save him a bit of the cream.

Tarla finished her chicken, licked her lips, and headed straight back towards the gaping wound she had made in the black bin bag, but as she scrambled back up the easily scaled, haphazardly stacked rubbish, she succeeded in unsettling the top piece of the jigsaw. A bulging sack of bottles began to cascade downwards, causing an avalanche to follow. Glass exploded everywhere on impact, and Evil screamed out loudly as he received a blow to the head. Both mother and son, fur standing to attention in fright, made their escape as the shattering noise continued to echo all around. Walls were climbed with one major bound as Tarla and Evil disappeared at breakneck speed to find sanctuary elsewhere.

And as a deathly silence descended all around, nothing moved. The yard was now a total mess, but no humans appeared, so Giblet thought it might be safe to climb down from the heady heights as his neck was now hurting and his feet were very sore. Both mice clambered down into the littered yard and silently moved and hid behind the many obstacles lying all around. It was an ideal situation for them, as Chester headed straight for the last remnants of Evil's cake and tentatively licked at the gritty cream, whilst Giblet got his hard-earned reward as his head and his body disappeared into a cavernous chicken carcass. He would not be seen for a while. Chester quickly tired of spitting out his glassy treat and moved onto a multi-coloured mountain that had appeared nearby. A ham sandwich received a huge bite, but Chester's eyes swivelled in their sockets as a pickled onion was quickly expelled from his mouth. Maybe he would have better luck with those strawberries, and he did; they were delicious and the sugar was divine. He settled down to gorge himself and quickly forgot about what had occurred just a few moments before.

An hour passed by very quickly and the grey clouds had disappeared and taken their watery load elsewhere. The sun now dominated the sky and a visible steam rose from the ground and the rooftops, as Anfield dried out. Giblet continued with his meal; his initial chomping was now a nibble, and Chester, who had visited every possible food source and tasted the lot, was now feeling fully sated. His belly bulged and his movements slowed; he needed a drink quickly as a mighty burp brought back the taste of the pickled onion.

Chester surveyed the scene and his eyes suddenly trained on an overturned box of bottles. He decided it needed investigating and as he dragged his bloated body forward, he wished he hadn't been such a pig, even though he was a mouse. Chester's stomach gently pressed against the broken glass, but some bottles had half survived and still yielded a colourful liquid, and with no caution shown and no hesitation either, Chester plunged his tongue straight into one of the trapped pools and quickly retracted it as the first bitter taste hit home. He shook his head violently from side to side, his eyes shut tightly and his cheeks sucked in and puffed out as he tried to decide whether he liked the taste or not. Another lap told him that he did, and he quickly drank some more. Chester did not know what it was that he was drinking but he thought to himself, if only he could read, surely that dangling label would say elderberry wine.

The last droplets of liquid vanished as Chester's tongue tired, and with his thirst now fully quenched he slowly retreated out of his glass watering hole, and into the now bright sunlight. As the powerful rays attacked his eyes, Chester squinted for protection. His front left leg gave way to a little wobble and then his right leg followed suit, and Chester's chin hit the ground with a mighty thud. "What was that?" Chester thought to himself, but it was his only thought, as his mind, now muddled and clouded, rapidly closed down. Chester, with his collapse now total, lay there spread-eagled and began to snore.

Giblet now returned to ground, well fed and satisfied. He called out for his pal but there was no answer, only the nasally rumblings of a deep sleeper replied. Chester was out for the count and Giblet quickly realised why, as he sniffed closely at Chester's breath and recoiled, for the slumped and wretched figure before him was as drunk as drunk could be. "Oh no," Giblet thought, "how can I get him out of here," as a brief moment of panic washed over him. He could not leave Chester exposed like this, as the sun continued to beat down and Tarla might also return. Giblet took Chester's long skinny tail in his mouth and somehow managed to drag him over to the shaded corner of the yard, and with his legs splayed in all directions, the prostrate Chester slept on and on and on. Little gurgling noises escaped from his mouth, and his jaws chattered together with every breath.

Giblet lay there for over two hours and fought a continuous battle to keep his eyes open as he guarded his pal, for that is what friends do. And it was just as well that he had won that fight, for what now ambled into view shocked him to the very core and set his heart a pounding as the trembling returned. News and smells travel fast when there is a feast to be had, and this uninvited guest was not welcome. The rat, almost as big as a cat, chased all thoughts of Chester's welfare far from Giblet's mind as his own self-preservation mode kicked in. With lightning speed and in one movement Giblet rose to his feet, ran and forcibly pushed himself headlong into the man-made rubbish mountain and disappeared. He hoped he hadn't been spotted by the new intruder on the scene. He hadn't but he had been heard. The rat as big as a cat reared up onto his powerful hind legs, and with his huge body now supported by his equally powerful tail, sniffed the air and sniffed some more. It was at this point that Giblet, who now peered out from his cornflake box hide, could see the enormity of the interloper before him. A huge head accompanied the huge body and large brown coloured daggers sat neatly in Ratty's mouth, and these weapons were not for show. A long streak of white fur in the shape of a flash emblazoned the right side of his long, thin face, a face to frighten other rats – it was certainly frightening Giblet. Newly-named Flash now felt that he could relax and settle down, and, as a corn on the cob beckoned him, he began to feed.

Chester's left eye started to open but his right eye refused as the fallen mouse began to stir. His head and his legs were still positioned like a bearskin rug. "What am I? Where am I? Who am I?" were the first thoughts that raced through his head, alongside a thumping headache. Chester, with great difficulty, got to his feet. A feeble groan that sounded very much like an "ooh" and an "aah" involuntarily escaped from his mouth. He shook his head but wished he hadn't, and as his blood-shot eyes tried to focus, he imagined he could see two brown rats with white stripes merge into one. Flash had only half finished his corn when a strong odour invaded his nostrils; it smelt very much like peanut butter, a particular favourite of his. He began to sniff furiously up and down, but kept returning to the one spot. The disturbed rubbish had obviously spread it from its original source. He knew it was close by, but where?

As ever, Chester's timing left a lot to be desired as a loud hiccup exploded from his throat. The startled Flash turned quickly to his left, and in his haste, stumbled into a rusty tin can. His mighty tail swished and an almighty thwack broke the silence, as Flash leapt three feet into the air. Chester now saw that imaginary rat in flight. Two graceful somersaults and a back flip later Flash landed softly back to earth and alongside the cornered Chester. Chester now stared death in the face; he was trembling and stiff at the same time. He had a dry mouth and was sweating heavily as his four months of life whizzed by before him, and with his eyes shut tightly, he awaited his fate. Flash or Rat or whatever he was called now had the mouse at his mercy. He could deliver the bite required at any time of his choosing, but he didn't. He just turned away from Chester, and looked back at the peanut buttered killer trap. Flash quickly disappeared through a hole in the leaning wall. The fortunate Chester had been spared yet again.

Giblet and Chester had had enough excitement for one day. They scrambled back up the broken door, squeezed through the knotless holes, and then went their separate ways, back home to safety. Chester clambered back through the broken air brick and climbed the bare stairs. He dropped through the split in the old floorboards that led underneath the disused toilets. He could now see the welcoming sight of his bed of straw and paper inviting him in. He wasted no time at all as he collapsed exhausted in a heap and fell fast asleep.

Chester slept on throughout the whole of the next day; his slumbers were only broken by the sounds of humans banging and shouting in the derelict rooms above. He felt awful. His head was still thumping and his belly rumbled and bubbled within. He convinced himself that it was because of something he had eaten. But amongst his occasional awakenings he wondered to himself where Giblet was, as it was very strange that he hadn't called around for me.

Giblet had been doing a lot of thinking himself. He had been out and about as usual the day Chester slept but he had not called around for him. A second day soon passed and Chester was back to his usual self. He felt great as he waited for Giblet to call, but he waited and waited until he could wait no longer, for he was now starving.

Chester dropped down into the alleyway and decided to go and look for his very best friend, but instead of going to his left, the only way he had ever been, he turned to his right, for he knew Giblet's haunts were in that direction. He set off more in hope for he knew not where his chosen route would lead him too. His ears began to scrutinise the air waves for the slightest of sounds. The smells of a few days previously had all disappeared, and now there were soapy suds where the bin bags had once sat.

All thoughts of food were now secondary as Chester ploughed on in search of his pal, for he was now really worried about him, but then he remembered Giblet saying that it only took him about five minutes to reach his house, so it couldn't be that far. A few moments later Chester came alongside a backyard with the door wide open – nothing unusual in that – but he could hear a distant noise from within. He stepped inside so he could take a closer look. Huddled in a small group at the other end of the yard, six or seven mice whom Chester had never seen before ravenously devoured whatever it was they were ravenously devouring. They were oblivious to Chester's presence. But amongst the gluttonous throng there was one shape that Chester did recognise. The smallest mouse at the far end of the dinner table could only be, and it was, Giblet.

Chester called out excitedly as a feeling of relief swept over him. For he now knew that Giblet was safe and well. Seven mouse heads immediately turned to face Chester; their mouths were stuffed full to the brim, and Chester knew from the steely stares that returned his gaze that he was not welcome. Chester expected a quick response from Giblet, a sign of recognition of some sort, but it was not forthcoming. Instead Giblet stood there for a few moments in a trance-like state, as if not knowing how he should react. He then quickly swallowed his tasty mouthful, although he couldn't taste it at all, and turned back towards his dinner guests and encouraged them to finish their meal. Giblet breathed deeply, a sign that he was building up his courage. He now turned and moved slowly towards where Chester was standing.

"Hiya, Giblet!" Chester shouted out loudly as he gleefully greeted his friend, "I have been really worried about you. Where have you been?" Chester asked as he wrapped his arms around his mate and hugged him tightly. Giblet broke free from Chester's embrace and ushered him quickly outside into the alleyway, as six mice who hadn't returned to their meal intruded on the scene, for they knew what was about to happen. Something slowly dawned on Chester as he solemnly asked of his pal, "What's up, Giblet, is there something wrong?" There was. Giblet swallowed hard. He half-looked Chester in the eyes before his gaze drifted towards the ground as he announced in a faltering voice.

"I won't be able to see you anymore, Chester." There, it was said. Giblet had struggled all of the previous day with his emotions and with these thoughts. "Am I doing the right thing? How will it affect Chester?" But it was too late to worry about it now for the deed was done. Chester stood there open mouthed, taken aback by what he thought he had just heard. He slightly shook his head and then he quietly uttered the question,

"What do you mean, Giblet? What do you mean?" Chester received his response, but it was not to his liking. Giblet did not hold back as he cruelly delivered his reply.

"I won't be able to see you anymore. It's far too dangerous to be with you. It used to be a laugh, but it isn't now. You are going to get us killed. I can't look out for both of us any longer. You are too much of a scatterbrain and I want no more of it," Giblet concluded and then broke off from his rant. The shocked and bewildered Chester could find no words; there was now only a silence as both rodents looked deep into each other's eyes. There wasn't anything else to be said, and Giblet slowly turned and walked away leaving Chester with his thoughts.

A few moments later Chester also turned to walk away, or rather slunk, as his shoulders hung low almost touching the ground. There had never been such a forlorn figure before. The realisation of his situation now hit home, and hit home hard. He had never felt like this before; he felt so sad, so very, very sad. Chester continued his slink with his head bowed, back down the alleyway and disappeared. Giblet was now feeling really guilty and raced back to the open door and shouted out in Chester's direction,

"Look after yourse…" He was unable to finish his sentence, for Chester was now gone.

## 3   A Terrible Loss

It was now another baking hot day and the sun beat down relentlessly. Chester was hungry and still feeling sad as he seemingly shuffled aimlessly down the cobbled alleyway. He also felt he was all alone in the world. His mum had told him to leave, and a friend had told him he was not welcome anymore. How much more confused can an already confused mouse become? Chester made his way towards Mrs. Jones's yard at no 24, and hoped the little old lady would be at home. He settled down in his usual spot where he knew he could be seen from the dusty paned window. Mrs. Jones's house had seen better days; time and the elements had taken their toll on the once neat family home, but now all she could do was to sit and watch as she witnessed its continuous decay. It didn't take long for Mrs. Jones, who was also very lonely, to appear with fruit cake in hand. She called out her usual chant of "Hello, little

Mousie," and "How are you today, little Mousie," as she broke up and scattered her wares. She watched contentedly as Chester scooped up a raisin in his little hands and nibbled furiously. It was the highlight of Mrs. Jones's day, and it made Chester feel that he was not totally on his own in this dangerous world, as he greedily devoured chunk after chunk.

The now full Chester grabbed at the last piece of cake and decided he would store it for later. He then turned on his heels and slid effortlessly under the gap beneath the backyard door and back out into the cobbled passage. There was no thank-you from Chester to Mrs. Jones. No, she had already had her pleasure as she returned indoors to continue with her lonely existence.

With a sudden jolt and a heavy thud to his side, the hoarded fruit cake was ejected quickly from Chester's mouth; it rolled over and over and came to rest on the greasy cobbles. The well fed and unwary Chester had slid effortlessly under the gap of the backyard door and straight into Tarla. With a sudden pounce and a swat of the paw, Chester found himself trapped in a prison of claws. The ground almost immediately disappeared beneath him, as in only two, but lightning quick movements Tarla, with Chester held firmly in her mouth, landed in another yard. Her paws felt light to Chester, not as heavy as he would have imagined as they rested on top of his submissive body. Tarla's head lowered as she sniffed at Chester; her slitty eyes of green loomed large. The first flight up into the air came as a bit of a shock to Chester's system as Tarla gently batted him skywards. The second was immensely enjoyable and exhilarating as the airborne Chester let out a cry of delight. Tarla must be a friendly cat, Chester thought to himself, as a whoopee escaped his lips. A second and a third whoopee alerted Giblet who just happened to be passing. He knew those excited screams off by heart. He quickly peered under the gap beneath the backyard door, and now his horror was complete, as he watched the flying Chester enjoying his torture. Chester's face now began to turn a different colour, as the repeated hurls upwards were now making him wish they would stop and stop quickly. His whoopees had now turned to stifled "urghs", as his cheeks puffed out and his tightly shut mouth suppressed the rising fruit cake within.

Giblet had to act very quickly and act he did. With no thought for his own safety, he raced out from under his cover to try and distract the now bored Tarla. Chester hit the ground hard as Tarla rushed forward towards the mocking Giblet, who shouted to Chester to *"RUN!"* and Chester ran. Giblet easily avoided Tarla's first swipe, but he did not notice Evil's approach from behind, and with a tremendous speed the novice killer struck, pinning Giblet with his teeth. As Giblet's tormented screams reached his ears, the shocked Chester burst into tears. For Giblet, the greatest friend anyone could have, died that day.

# 4  The Journey

Chester tossed and turned and hardly slept in his bed of paper and straw. He hadn't eaten for two days as all of his thoughts were of his friend's demise, of the ultimate sacrifice paid by Giblet to save a foolish mouse. Chester scolded himself repeatedly. What had happened was the talk of Anfield, as word quickly spread amongst all of the other mice. Maisie, realising her son's predicament, tried to comfort him and brought some food. He couldn't eat, and refused her offerings. He just lay there listlessly as the newly born siblings watched from afar. They could also sense Chester's grief and left him well alone.

Another day quickly elapsed and Chester took a tentative nibble at a broken biscuit. He had hardly munched his first munch when all hell broke loose. The black dusty space that had long been his sanctuary suddenly exploded into a deafening noise, and bright light speared the century old darkness, as an army of builders attacked the large Victorian house in St. Domingo vale.

Floorboards felt the force of the hammer and were reduced to six-foot splinters, as the electricians went to work. The miles of spaghetti wiring that many a mouse had gnawed were now ripped out and discarded. Suddenly a human voice boomed out with an ear-splitting scream, "Mice! Mice! And loads of them!" Eight burly tradesmen rushed to the scene. In the disused toilet there was now mayhem as the men smashed down erratically with whatever they had in hand, and a hundred mice fled for their lives. The noise jolted Chester back to reality and he quickly bounded out of bed. The shouting and screaming and laughing were many a mouse's saving grace, as the wild humans hysterically made light of the serious situation, allowing almost all to escape.

Chester quickly scaled a joist and, without thinking, jumped into what he thought was a safe haven. It wasn't, and he quickly realised this as he slipped further down inside the small metal box. A screwdriver shifted and pinned Chester fast, and a spring-loaded tape sprang out and connected. Chester had only gone and done it again, for he was now trapped in a tool-box prison. Chester began to struggle and struggled some more, but it was all to no avail. He tired very quickly and abandoned the fight. Three days of fasting had now taken its toll. More weight was added as tools were taken from and returned to the box, as the now calm builders continued with their work.

Maisie sniffed at the grill and sensed Chester's fear, but there was nothing she could do to help her stricken son. She could now also sense the workmen's return, so she reluctantly ran for cover. Maisie watched as the last tools were packed away and the large electrician retrieved his box and made his way down the bare stairs and out of the house. She caught her last sight of Chester's tomb as it was packed away into the back of a large white van. Doors were quickly slammed shut with a loud metallic clang, and then, as the engine kicked into life, it was off in a cloud of dust and screeching brakes. Maisie could just about make out the sign emblazoned on the sides of the electrician's van. In huge black letters were the words: **LES. S. SHOCKS**.

There was no movement from Chester as the long journey continued, for he couldn't move and, with every bump the van negotiated, the screwdriver pressed a little deeper, the sharp edges of the metal tape threatened to cut him and the roar of the powerful engine added to his woes. Chester began to reflect on his short four months of life, the scrapes he had gotten himself and others into and the many pranks he had played. He thought of the poisoned bait, the red liquid, the rats and the cats, Mrs. Jones and the woman with the bleached blond hair with the black stripe down the middle. He thought of mum, his siblings, and his father Handsome Ted, and then there was Giblet, and now this. Chester was on the verge of giving up. He slowly closed his eyes, hoping he would wake up and this would all be a bad dream. He didn't care anymore, he just wished his misfortunes would soon end.

Les. S. Shocks took the bend in the road in Renacres Lane, Southport, far too fast as his van lurched over onto two wheels. He braked hard and furiously wrestled with the steering and just about managed to save himself from disaster. Shattering and clattering and banging noises escaped from the back of the van, and as all the tools righted themselves as the vehicle came to a halt, the startled Chester was now free – not from the box, but from the penetrating jab of the screwdriver, and the restrictive tape measure. He took deep gulps of air, his heart pounded, but he felt a little better. Les. S. Shocks also took deep gulps of air as he gathered his composure before continuing with his journey. He hadn't far to go now, but he made sure he drove a lot more slowly.

Shortly afterwards the van came to a stop. A key entered the lock and the back doors swung open wide, Les surveyed the mess within and decided to leave it be, but he yanked out the small tool box and retired into his smart Southport home. Chester felt the warm air of the hallway, but smelt something nasty as Les kicked off his boots. He tried to kiss his wife, Tanya, but all she was interested in was to hurriedly shepherd Les into the kitchen and tell him to remove his smelly socks. Chester could now feel the cooler air of that room as Les dumped the metal box unceremoniously down on the floor. He could now also smell a familiar scent that he knew only too well, for Les and Tanya were the proud owners of cats, two of them, in fact. They were fat and bloated, not at all like the sleek felines of Anfield. Mowser and Towser were the not so original names that Les and Tanya had come up with. The two cats excitedly greeted their master but quickly broke away and shifted their attention to the box and began to sniff.

Les devoured Tanya's prepared meal, oblivious to Mowser and Towser's prolonged interest in his tools. He let out a sizeable burp, patted his outsize belly, and then retired from the room, leaving his dishes for someone else to clear away.

"Goodnight, Mowser. Goodnight, Towser," he shouted out, as he switched off the lights and closed the kitchen door behind him.

Chester endured one of the worst nights of his life, as he huddled petrified and out of his wits in the corner of his cell. He didn't want to break out as the cats were trying to break in. They scratched and purred and scratched some more, and in their frustration, they found the strength to slide the box around the room. Mowser and Towser eventually gave up for the night, but as soon as first light came, they were back to torment the hapless Chester. Les, empty cup in hand, yawned loudly and stretched his other arm high above his head. He climbed out of his bed and went downstairs. He opened the creaky kitchen door, and greeted his pets with a hearty good morning. The tired cats hardly moved and hardly noticed Les as they continued to eagerly monitor their prey. Les now noticed their interest as both cats salivated over the box and refused to budge; their years of easy living hadn't dulled their instincts.

"What's up, Mowser, something in there, is there? Something in my box?" Les enquired, not really expecting an answer, but he got one all the same, because Mowser and Towser raised themselves from their crouched positions, and with their heads now towering above the metal container, they began to swish their tails from side to side. Les was now very interested himself, as he ventured forward and nervously lifted the tool box lid, not knowing what he would find inside. His eyes rapidly scanned the many shapes but nothing untoward stood out. He moved the tape measure and there it was, a pathetic brown ball of fur that cowered low and far too weak to move, now came into view.

Chester slightly stirred as his room became awash with light. He was exposed and feeling very vulnerable. Did he care? He didn't know. He just lay there. Chester and Les's eyes now met, as Mowser and Towser were grabbed by the scruffs of their necks as they eagerly tried to be first to get to their quarry. Both cats now got the message Les was sending, as he gently tossed them towards their beds, and they then landed as moggies do, on all fours. Les reached in and carefully lifted the weary mouse out of the cold metal chamber and placed him onto his blister-ridden palm. Chester felt an immediate warmth as a large finger softly caressed up and down the length of his body. His fur ruffled and a nice relaxing sensation swept over him, as Les's voice, gentle for such a big man, encouraged the poorly mouse to revive. Chester lay there motionless and absorbed the heat from Les's large hand. The warmth flowed freely through his body and reached his cold bones. Should he move, he thought to himself. Could he move, he thought to himself. Could he trust this human as he had trusted Tarla as he flew through the air – look what had happened then.

The caressing finger continued to caress ever so gently the length of his now relaxed frame. The stiffening had surrendered and given way to a pleasurable contentment, and Chester began to make soft murmuring sounds. Mowser and Towser made noises too, but they weren't soft murmuring sounds as they sat rigidly at Les's feet, their piercing eyes frozen as they impatiently begged Les to notice them. The quiet of that early hour was interrupted and the peaceful calm quickly disappeared as Les suddenly asked a question of his furry friends.

"What's up, Mowser, want a fresh mouse for breakfast, do you? You too, Towser, want a fresh mouse?"

Mowser and Towser now stood to attention, and simultaneously meowed with their yellowed teeth bared. Chester's eyelids parted and his eyes exploded back to life, as Les hoisted him high and started to dangle him by the tail. The cruel man slowly swished his captive from left to right, up and down, as if trying to hypnotise the hopeful cats who now greedily surveyed the overdue prize.

"Who shall have it?" Les enquired as a devilish grin creased his face. "I've only got one mouse and there are two of you." Les theatrically let out a sinister laugh. Mowser and Towser now gulped, as Les suspended the frail mouse closer and closer to them, Chester knew the next gulp could mean the end of him and started to pray.

Suddenly a voice boomed out, much louder than the mayhem already in progress down below, as Tanya shouted from the top of the stairs and at the top of her voice.

"Les, what's going on down there, I can't sleep."
Les turned sharply. The big man was momentarily distracted as he weakly called back in a blustering voice,

"Erh, nothing, my dear, I am making you a nice cup of tea." Chester had to seize his opportunity, and so he did as he took advantage of Les's lapse in concentration. Summoning up all of his last reserves of energy, the hungry mouse reared up sharply and bit the unsuspecting Les hard on his finger. Blood spurted immediately from the once-friendly digit, as the large man, who had now shown he was really a small man, screamed and hopped about whilst dropping Chester to the floor.

Mowser and Towser both pounced together as Chester made his bid for freedom. Their large heads collided with an almighty thud, as the years of inactivity proved decisive and clouded their judgement. Chester escaped under the washing machine without a moment to spare as the dazed cats rejoined the hunt.

Les dunked his wounded finger under the fast-flowing tap. He ranted and he cursed and stamped his feet up and down, as he held his throbbing joint tightly, almost crying as he reached for a plaster. Now he was angry as he pushed Mowser and Towser firmly out of the way and violently maneuvered the washing machine out from under the work tops and into the open. Chester had managed to climb high up into the innards of Tanya's valued friend, and as much as Les thumped and turned the machine unceremoniously onto its side, Chester held on tightly.

Tanya suddenly appeared, and her posh Southport accent seemed to disappear as she screamed out loudly, taking Les unawares.

"What are you doing with my machine, you *stupid* man! Leave it alone, put it back right now." Les came up with a weak reply, something about a leak and that he had fixed it, whilst pointing to his open tool box to back up his claim. This seemed to pacify the touchy wife, as he quickly responded to her request and replaced the bruised appliance. Les fidgeted throughout the day, his finger still throbbed and continuously reminded him that he had a mouse in the house. Mowser and Towser lay there thoroughly frustrated, and Tanya interrupted Chester's sleep continuously as Les's shirts and socks swirled around and around in a soapy sea. The day seemed to drag, as Tanya carried on with her chores. The cats were ousted out into the yard and did what cats do best, and made a mess of the next door neighbour's garden. Les had a beer, had a bet, and then had a sleep.

Three o'clock in the morning arrived and Les and Tanya had long since gone to bed and the cats had returned through the flap ready for some rest themselves. Their snores now invited Chester to climb down from his safe haven and explore his surroundings. His broken sleep had, in fact, done him a power of good, but now what he needed most was a good meal. Almost four days had passed since his last feed, which must have been some sort of record for a mouse; it certainly was for him. Chester slowly approached the large cat bowl that he could smell rather than see, as it was very dark; only a dim light on the front of the fridge freezer offered any kind of illumination. Chester could feel the heat from Towser's fishy breath; he slept soundly with his head by the side of his dish. Chester's senses identified a huge chunk of food; he didn't know what it was, he just grabbed at it. He wasn't choosy, he was just hungry; it fitted neatly between his teeth and accompanied Chester back to his hide. Chester had never tasted tuna before but he quite liked it as he visited the dish a further twenty-five times that night. The food disappeared and Chester cheekily drank some of the cat's water as well.

Tanya came downstairs in the morning and remarked to Les, "Those cats must have been hungry as they've finished off all of their food." One day passed, two days passed and a third morning arrived. Tanya commented to Les, "Maybe we should increase the cats' food as they are obviously starving."

# 5  Strange New World

Chester was now the picture of health. His bony frame had once again been covered with ample flesh; it was now time for him to make his move as it was far too dangerous to stay here anymore, he thought to himself. But he didn't just move. No, Chester stayed where he was, for something inside his brain had suddenly clicked. He pondered his situation as he now began to reflect once more on the past few weeks and everything that had happened to him in that time. There was an absence of the impulsiveness that had made him leap into everything he did without looking first. Chester the mouse, who seemed to have had twenty-six lives, and who seemed to have misfortune for a middle name, had now acquired what he needed most – awareness. An awareness coupled with his newly found maturity told him, no, and stopped him from leaving his electric shelter. He bided his time and analysed his situation right down to the last detail. He was well fed, so he would have plenty of energy to call upon if needed. The cats were outside in the garden, or someone else's. He would run like the wind if spotted; he wouldn't just stand there. He would make his moves early and not hang around, but be prepared to change the plan if need be. Chester could not believe he was having all of these thoughts flooding into his brain, and he seemed to have plenty of room for more. Chester the adventurous mouse had apparently grown up, many months late maybe, but better late than never.

It was now time for Chester to act and he did. All was quiet as he crept along the cold tiled floor and sniffed the air. The cat flap would need to be overcome but with lots of caution, as Chester had witnessed its guillotine potential over the past few days. One small leap and he was there. He balanced precariously as he peered out of the smallest of gaps. Mowser and Towser were sleeping in the shade of the large oak tree. A fluffy ball lying beside them told Chester that they had had their fun. Brown leaves littered the ground all around. "Good," Chester thought to himself, "same colour as me. That will help," and out he went.

A large smoking factory chimney towered high above Les's small house. Chester thought, "I can squeeze through the fence and make for that." Everything was going to plan, the leaves were providing the perfect foil, the grass was cut very short and aided his speed, and the wind was blowing in the right direction. His smell never reached the cats' nostrils. Chester's plan had only one teeny-weeny flaw in it, for he hadn't reckoned on Tanya appearing with her laundry basket in hand and screaming:

"*Mice, Mice, Mice!*" at the top of her voice, whilst jumping up onto the garden chair as the washing took flight, and Les's newly cleaned underpants landed on her head.

Mowser and Towser now stood to attention as Tanya's shrieks continued to pierce the air. Both the cats now ran around in different directions, trying to impress Tanya and make out that they were really top cats. They stumbled and they fumbled, and you know what, they found and cornered Chester, more by luck rather than by stealth. Chester now fixed his stare on his hostile opponents as the cats edged closer. This was the moment the daft mouse from Anfield had to stand tall and be counted. He had to show bravery, and confront what a million mice had faced before him. Cat versus mouse, an historic encounter, a daunting task maybe, but not one where the cat was always guaranteed to win, and Chester was determined that that would be the case here. It had to be. An inner strength rose from within as Chester puffed out his chest and concentrated his gaze beyond his approaching foes. He had a major advantage in his favour as he spotted the small gap in the fence, for the two fat cats in front of him were not

Tarla and Evil. Those feral warriors could show Mowser and Towser a thing or two. With a speed he never knew he had, Chester side stepped and wrong footed the dozy twosome, as they lashed out together and swiped the fresh air. Chester was through the gap and made good his retreat. He left his pursuers in his wake as they struggled to climb the fence.

Mowser and Towser slowly but surely closed the distance between them and their intended victim. Chester's small legs couldn't compete with their longer bounds, and the uneven ground of the cheese factory was starting to take its toll. Poor Chester's lungs were now close to bursting. He slowed rapidly as he reached the dump and a hole loomed large. Could he make it? He had to. He did, but only just. Success, almost but not quite. Mowser's barbed paw thrust deep inside the small opening and missed by a matter of inches as Chester fell in exhausted and felt the downhill ground disappear beneath him. He rolled and he rolled out of control, and out of Mowser's reach. The air was thick with dust, as the heavy cats' momentum carried them forward and destroyed the entrance to the mound. They then began to fight each other furiously as they jostled for a peep. The dust took an age to settle and when it did, Chester could still see Mowser's face at the opening, blocking out the light. Mowser snorted and threatened, as he could also see the untouchable Chester.

Chester felt something close to him and climbed back to his feet and then off his feet, as a large hand lifted him high into the air. The largest mouse he had ever seen stood before him and held him aloft. The largest mouse Chester had ever seen had a red cap and wore an even redder coat. He had a very menacing look.

"Who are you? What are you?" the oversized door attendant in the fancy dress demanded to know as he frog-marched Chester roughly through the haze and back up the hill. Chester, still gasping for breath and with his heart still thumping rapidly, screeched out in desperation:

"I am Chester. My name is Chester," as he pleaded to be let go. His ejection continued and was almost complete as his pleas fell on deaf ears, and Mowser's face began to loom large again.

Suddenly a voice screamed out and stopped the burly bouncer, I mean commissionaire, in his tracks.

"*ROBARTS, ROBARTS*, put him down," the voice angrily demanded, but Robarts refused to relent as he took another step forward. "*ROBARTS, ROBARTS*, do as I say, and put him down now."

Robarts turned quickly and Chester was swung around with him and faced the source of all the instructions, and there she was. Chester's already fast beating heart skipped a beat and pounded faster and faster. The most beautiful mouse he had ever seen stood there before him. She had jet black fur with a shiny sheen.

Chester wished he was more of a romantic, so that he could adequately describe her lovely eyes. She was wearing a beautiful white gown that added to her elegance. Chester wondered to himself, what this world was, that he had stumbled into, red caps and coats, mice in beautiful clothes.

The lady stood her ground and faced up to her defiant opponent; her eyes were unflinching. She meant what she had said. Robarts reluctantly gave way first, and dropped the dangling Chester to the floor.

"I shall inform Victor of this, and see what he has to say. There will be trouble!" Robarts protested loudly and off he stormed, whilst brushing the dirt from his coat.

Chester thought he could hear the lady calling to him, but he didn't react. He just stood there looking at her, totally mesmerised and in a trance, and also his ears were full of muck so that didn't help. A soft hand bearing a tissue slowly rose up and gently wiped the soil from Chester's brow, sending a sensation Chester had never felt before rushing through his body. It was a warm glowing pleasant feeling that swept over him at breakneck speed, head to toe and back again. His heart pounded and his head throbbed, but he liked what was happening to him and he wanted more, for there was now no doubt, LITTLE CHESTER WAS IN LOVE. The sounds of "Please come with me. Please come now," had no place in Chester's pleasurable thoughts, but those words suddenly invaded his mind and brought him back to his senses. The outstandingly attractive woman continued with her urgings, and began to drag Chester by the hand.

"We must move quickly and get you cleaned up. Follow me," she ordered in a much quieter voice, as she now had Chester's full attention. "Victor will be here soon, so now let's go," she continued and led the way as they descended deeper underground and into the bowels of the man-made rubbish mountain. Chester didn't need much persuasion to follow this beauty, as he spat out a mouthful of grit and called out loudly,

"Who's Victor?" There was no reply, apart from a whispered,

"shush, keep moving".

Chester and his companion swept past at least twenty-seven other mice as they continued to wherever it was they were going to.

All of the mice had clothes or costumes on and all asked the same questions, "What's happening and who is he?" adding, "There will be trouble," and, "Victor won't be very happy." Chester, although covered from head to toe with dust, felt naked in their presence.

Eventually they reached the very bottom of the mound, and in the hollow that appeared before them, a warm pool of water with steam rising from it came into view. Chester had never seen anything like it and he excitedly asked the lady, "Is it magic?"

To this she replied, "No, it's just a leak from the hot water pipe above!"

Chester felt very scruffy and didn't need much prompting to get in and have a good scrub, and rid himself of his gritty suit. But before he did, he asked the lovely female her name.

"Arrabella," came the reply, as she turned her back and told Chester to hurry up and get in and have a wash. Now Chester did not know if mice liked water or not, or whether they ducked and dived, but this one certainly did as he frolicked about, and water cascaded this way and that. It was another new sensation to him; it wasn't like this in Anfield, he thought as he shook himself dry.

Arrabella turned and faced Chester. She was just about to say something but couldn't. The words became trapped in her throat, as she caught sight of Chester's now clean face. Handsome Ted's looks were now Chester's looks, and Arrabella was now feeling what Chester had felt ten minutes previously. Their eyes met and without much thought and very little restraint, they moved towards each other. They couldn't help themselves as powerful feelings of wanting surged through their bodies.

A booming voice exploded in the silence, stopping the lovelorn rodents in their tracks, and the shocked pair quickly turned towards the untimely interrupter.

"There they are. I told you so!" Robarts screamed out loudly, reaffirming what he had already told the closely-following Victor.

Victor was even bigger than Robarts. He looked like a half mouse, half rat. He was massive and dressed in a military uniform, like a Russian soldier. He looked menacing as he pushed Robarts out of the way and marched resolutely towards Chester. Not a word was said, but there were plenty of oohs and ahhs and oh nos from the hidden audience, as Victor lashed out at Chester, sending him backwards, back into the warm bath, and sending Arrabella into an uncontrolled rage, as she violently thumped at Victor's chest.

"Why did you do that? Why? He wasn't doing anything wrong!" she screamed as she continued to scold Victor. Robarts grabbed hold of the distraught female from behind. Her dress was now crumpled, and her legs flailed wildly, as she was hoisted off the ground.

Victor didn't look bothered in the slightest as he told her, "You know we don't allow strangers in this place."

Victor barked out two more orders, one to the bloodied Chester to get out of the water and one to Robarts to get rid of him. Victor turned on his heels, and as he did, his well-honed sword rattled as it caught the floor. Robarts followed him like a lost puppy as he passed down Victor's orders to a lesser soldier. Arrabella, crying and confused, now ran pleading in Victor's wake, begging him to reconsider his decision and allow Chester to stay.

"He could be useful here," She pleaded. She screamed, she shouted, but it seemed it was all to no avail as Victor strode on. Arrabella was now extremely agitated as the panic she was experiencing totally overwhelmed her. She had nothing left to give, as she slumped to the floor and sobbed uncontrollably.

It was a lone dissenting voice at first who muttered quietly out of earshot of Victor, but a voice it was. One of the hidden audiences had ventured forth, dressed in a cowboy outfit with pearl-handled guns encased in a leather holster strapped to his side, and spluttered out the words, "Let him stay."

A mouse dressed like a nurse plucked up the same courage and joined the gunslinger and blurted out, "We want Chester. We want Chester, let him stay." The other twenty-seven mice whom Chester had passed previously, now all joined the throng, calling out in a disorganised way, but then in unison, as they gained in confidence. A loud crescendo built up and Chester's name reverberated loudly all around the irregular-shaped dome, sending particles of fine dust falling from the ceiling like rain.

"WE WANT CHESTER, WE WANT CHESTER, LET HIM STAY."

This was not really a rallying call on behalf of Chester, because the cowboy mouse hardly knew him. No, it was more a chance, an opportunity taken by all of these mice in silly costumes to show their smouldering resentment of Victor's dictatorial rule.

Victor's stride was broken, and he suddenly stopped, and then turned slowly. It was as if he had been hit from behind. His face mirrored his displeasure as he marched back towards the dissenters in his midst. There were more of the oohs and ahhs and the oh nos, as Victor purposefully closed the gap between them. Robarts followed closely behind, gleefully encouraging Victor's wrath.

Nearly all of the mice who had sought change now sought their hideaways, and ran for cover. Jessie James and Florence Nightingale stood firm. It was now or never. They held hands and held their breath and tried hard not to flinch. Victor towered menacingly over the pair, but although he wanted to, he didn't do anything, as his brain mulled over his next course of action. For even though he was a bully, he was also very clever, and he quickly realised that to lash out might not be the smartest move to keep control of these revolutionaries. The next few seconds seemed like an age for the two lone rebels. They could feel Victor's warm breath on their faces, and his eyes seemed to be burning right through them. Victor detected their nervousness and their quivering legs. He momentarily put them out of their misery as he turned towards Robarts and whispered in his ears. Robarts quickly disappeared and in next to no time, reappeared with a bright pink cloth in hand. Robarts thrust the material towards the drying Chester, and firmly told him to put it on if he was staying. Victor moved closer to Chester and told him in a gruff voice, "You will wear these at all times, and if I catch you without them there will be trouble. You won't find me so nice next time, and that goes for all of you!" he threatened, as his gaze scanned the fearful onlookers. Victor once more turned and went, forcibly dragging Arrabella with him. Chester moved as if he was about to interfere, but was held back for his own good.

Chester now picked up his pink attire and spread it out before him. *"I CAN'T WEAR THAT!"* he exclaimed loudly as he realised what it was.

"You must, you must!" came the unanimous reply as his new-found friends gently urged him to comply, or they would all be in serious trouble. "Now, please dress now," he was told.

Chester paused and paused some more before he picked the garment up, then quickly put it down again, but eventually he did what he was asked. A mouse in a clown's outfit zipped Chester up from behind, and his humiliation was now complete. Everyone tried their best not to laugh, but they couldn't help it as giggles resounded all around, for Chester, the brown ball of fur from a tough area of Liverpool, WAS NOW A PINK CAT. The thoroughly embarrassed Chester stood there as the mass huddle fell about in hysterics. Some were crying tears of joy, but eventually as the laughter subsided, some of the mice managed to regain control of themselves and tried to express a little sympathy for Chester, but a joker amongst them asked him if he would like some milk and the laughter started all over again.

The belittled Chester stood there and cast his eyes towards his artificial claws and his bushy tail. He was already feeling hot and bothered, and now he was feeling completely foolish. Everything was now getting to him as he angrily purred, I mean growled, "What is happening here? What is this place?" whilst trying to unzip the costume, but his curved claws hindered him.

Jessie James, Florence Nightingale, and the Jester encouraged Chester to sit down and they would try to explain. They told him that they all lived in fear of Victor and his cohorts, of how Victor thought he was a general, a real soldier. "He tells us of his many escapades, although the only army he has ever been involved with is an army of mice, raiding the corn stores on many a farm. He rules with an iron fist, and he keeps control by humiliating us at every opportunity, hence our clothes. We are beaten if we step out of line, and we are never allowed to venture outside, for we are all prisoners here. Arrabella is his property and she hates him so much, but she cannot escape. She is really nice, and helps us when she can."

An eager voice from behind interrupted all the explanations. It was a voice Chester found hard to understand, as he'd never heard an accent like it before. A fat mouse with his whiskers shaped like a moustache ventured forth, and Chester remarked, "He's got you dressed in a chef's costume then."

The bloated newcomer was taken aback by this remark. He felt slighted as he aggressively retorted, "No, this is not a a chef's costume as-a you putt-a it. *I am a real-a chef!* I am *Moussellini*, and I am-a from Italy. I do all-a the cooking here, but all I havv-a to cook-a with is-a the chees-a from the factory. Chees-a this an-a chees-a that, mouserela cheese, chees-a mousse, chees-a cake, I am-a as you say, sicka of eet. And all-a because Victor will only eat-a the chees-a."

Moussellini wasn't telling the whole truth though, because he also loved cheese. Moussellini continued with his rant, "So wadd-a I think-a when I hear-a you all-a shouting for cheese, I rush-a up a here to find it is-a nott-a the chees-a you ar-a shouting for-a. No, it is a Cheesta! We want-a Cheesta, it-a mak-a me so happy I could-a keese you!" And with that Mousellini scooped Chester the cat up into his huge arms and hugged him tightly.

Chester let out a phew and rejected the chef's advances as the strong whiff of parmesan invaded his nostrils. Mousellini put Chester down again and said he was returning to his kitchen. Florence called after him and asked what was for dinner. Mousellini didn't break his stride but gave a cheery wave, before replying, "It is-a supris-a." Everyone looked at each other and burst out laughing once again.

Dinner was eaten in silence; not one word was spoken. There was an air of fear all around as the mice all ate their cheese. Mousellini had done really well with the few ingredients available to him. Victor sat at the head of the table and stuffed himself as if food was going out of fashion, he roared loudly with laughter intermittently for no apparent reason. He seemed to be the only one who was enjoying himself. Arrabella sat at his side and winced. She just picked at her food whilst casting sneaking glances towards Chester – at least she thought it was Chester as she hadn't seen this cat before. Guards stood at every entrance to the canteen carrying out their duties, and Robarts ambled between the tables observing the diners, watching their every move. Chester could now feel the discomfort everyone else was experiencing and knew he would not like it here. His first fledgling thoughts of escape began to hatch.

# 6  The Escape

Over the next few days, the novelty of having a new face in the camp started to recede. As everyone carried on with their everyday chores, mostly cleaning and keeping the tunnels clear, all the mice seemed to walk about aimlessly as if in a robotic state. Victor had succeeded in stifling all the hopes and aspirations of his underlings, and they seemed to have reluctantly accepted this. There was no talk, no idle chatter or banter. Only the periodic orders from Robarts broke the silence. What a very sad existence they all live here, Chester thought to himself, as he wielded the brush he had been given and swept the never-ending dirt from the never-ending dirt floor.

Chester felt angry. He couldn't concentrate at all on what he had been told to do. All that kept going through his mind was that he wasn't meant to be doing this. He had been born in Anfield. He was and always had been a free mouse. He knew nothing but freedom. He wasn't born in some pet shop or cage. If he had been, he might have been able to accept his situation and what was happening to him much more easily. No, he was meant to be free, and free he would be.

Chester decided that he would seek Arrabella out and tell her of his plans and see if she would approve and maybe agree to go with him, but where could she be? "Where do I start?" he asked himself, as he did not know his way around this rubbish bunker. Chester started to question his subdued workmates about Arrabella's whereabouts, but many quickly shunned him and put some distance between Chester and themselves, whilst checking that they hadn't been spotted colluding thereby bringing the wrath of Victor down on them. Chester noticed Jessie James sitting all alone taking a rest and made his way over to him, pretending to sweep as he went. His eyes were sweeping also, looking out for any dangers and trying hard not to attract attention, which was very difficult for a pink cat.

"Hello, Jessie," Chester whispered as he began brushing under the bench. Jessie reluctantly lifted his feet to allow for the broom. "Would you know where Arrabella is? I need to find her as I am going to escape. Can you help me?" he asked and pleaded at the same time. Jessie sat up straight and became very interested in what was being said, as he too only had thoughts of freedom.

"I can help you, but I want to go too. You have to take me with you, is that okay?" The cowboy demanded to know. Chester readily agreed to this, but as yet, he told Jessie he hadn't formulated any plans, but when he had he would let him know. Jessie told Chester where Arrabella could be found, but impressed upon him the need to be very careful as she was always being watched very closely, and that he would find it very difficult to approach her.

Chester thanked Jessie for all of his help and promised once again that he would keep him informed of his next step, then turned to embark on his chosen route, but before he had gone more than a few feet, Jessie called him back and said in a rather exasperated way, "Can I tell you something, Chester?" Chester stood there quietly and listened, for he was all ears. "My name is not Jessie James as you keep calling me. My name is COMPASS, okay, Compass, that is my name!" the former Jessie stated emphatically.

Chester, feeling just a little bit perplexed but thoroughly chastened, stood there, surprised by the cowboy's angry protestations, before he quietly repeated in response, "Compass, your name is Compass. Okay I can live with that," and after a very short pause, he asked, "Why are you called Compass then?"

"Because I am very good with directions, and this will come in very useful if we manage to escape," Compass assured his new-found ally.

Chester remembered everything Giblet had taught him as he edged slowly down the dark tunnel and pressed himself hard up against its sides. His pink suit now had a red colouration to it. The winding passages seemed to go on forever as the lost mouse sought to find his way, but they didn't really go on forever. It was just that Chester was going around in circles. Eventually he heard some voices which led him to the clearing that Compass had described, and there she was. The lovely Arrabella with all her beauty stood there statuesque, and then sat down, as three female mice in pinafores gently brushed at her fur and repeatedly adjusted her clothing. They slavishly attended to what they thought was her every need as decreed by Victor, but this wasn't what she wanted – to be treated as if she was a queen. She looked decidedly bored as the three fusspots fussed around her. Chester was instantly mesmerised by the gorgeous figure before him, which had brought him to an immediate halt, as he admiringly continued with his gaze.

Chester then did his best to attract her attention. He waved his broom, he shushed and he squeaked, he blew air from his mouth with his cheeks puffed out. He ran out from his cover and then ran back in again, he jumped up, and he sat down, leapt about, and then he tripped over his bushy tail. That did the trick, as Arrabella and the three servants swung around in surprise when they heard the melée that the fallen Chester was making.

She rose slowly to her feet and at the same time motioned the maids to stop brushing her shiny black fur. Her gaze was unwavering as she began to walk tentatively forward, one slow step at a time.

"Is it you, Chester. Is it you?" she called as her speed increased, and she left the shocked trio in her wake. Chester regained his footing, and rushed forward with his arms outstretched, all caution was being thrown to the wind, as the besotted couple advanced towards each other. But just as Chester was about to take Arrabella in his arms, and deliver his first kiss, she thrust out her hands and stopped Chester's approach.

The bemused suitor stood there, taken aback by her sudden coldness and asked, "Don't you like me? Don't you want me?" There was no reply, as Arrabella took that one last step forward, looked Chester in the eyes, and then proceeded to lift the cat mask from his face. Arrabella's and Chester's muzzles now nuzzled each other's, and a long passionate kiss and embrace ensued. The two watching maids cooed and ahhed, as the third rushed from the scene.

Victor and Robarts were taken unawares as the agitated maid tried to force her way past the burly guardsmen blocking the way. They quickly swallowed the grapes they were munching and covered the chocolates and the cake. "Where was all the cheese then?" she thought to herself, for there was none to be seen as Victor called out to let her pass. The maid hurriedly blurted out every last detail of her story about what she had seen, and then begged for approval from her master, claiming "I did well didn't I, I did well?"

Victor got to his feet and pushed his chair firmly away from him; his face slowly changed colour as he looked down at the babbling informant at his feet and beckoned her to eat. Victor strode out of the room, picking up his sword as he went. Robarts gestured and twelve guards followed, there was a frightening feeling in the air. Someone would have to pay dearly for Victor's anger.

Chester and Arrabella had quickly exited from the clearing and made their way back up to the top of the tunnel for they knew there wasn't a moment to spare. Their lives were in grave danger. They had crossed the line. There could be no return. Compass was waiting for them as they emerged from out of the dusty hole. As word had spread fast and every last mouse had now joined him, ready for whatever eventuality may be about to happen. No encouragement was needed, for they were all united in their cause. It wasn't Chester's arrival that had sparked this revolt. No, he was just the trigger needed to prompt this long-delayed reaction to Victor's crude rule.

A mass hug ensued as everyone gleaned every last ounce of the courage they would need to face the impending confrontation, which moments later duly arrived. Victor got the surprise of his life as he surveyed the scene that greeted him. "These undersize underlings have the audacity to undermine me, to challenge my authority! They shall pay a heavy price," he thought to himself as he detected fear in their faces, for they were not trained fighters and would fall quickly. An invisible signal was given as Robarts, and now the seventeen soldiers who made up the full complement of Victor's army, marched forward to begin the attack. Fur flew, spit and blood too, as the violence erupted. Victor, like all bullies, stood by and watched from afar, for he reasoned that there was no need to get involved as his troops, although heavily outnumbered, seemed to be winning the day.

Arabella and the two maids joined in and did what women do. They pulled at fur, they scratched and screeched. It wasn't a pretty sight, and slowly but surely the tide began to turn. Something else was needed to completely turn the tables in Chester's beleaguered and ramshackle army's favour, and not a moment too soon it arrived. Mousellini stealthily sneaked up, spatula in hand, and crowned Robarts on top of his head. The fat mouse fell to the floor as the equally fat Mousellini sat on top of him. Victor was quickly overpowered without putting up much of a fight. The battle was now over, and loud cheers went up again and again and again.

Three mice, one dressed as a kangaroo, took Mousellini's place and sat on the struggling Robarts as the chef disappeared back to his kitchen, only to emerge soon after, pulling a large box behind him.

"Here," he shouted, "Tie their hands behind their backs with these, I never use them anyway."

Compass peered in and started the distribution. Victor and his clan were now bound so tightly with the cheese strings that they couldn't move an inch. The mercenary third maid now appeared and wanted to make her peace. She told Arabella and Chester of the vast hoard of food in Victor's apartments. There were biscuits and cakes, chocolates and sweets, "…for the cheese factory was not, as you have all been told, just a cheese factory."

They all ate well that evening and slept comfortably for the first time in ages. The next day everyone assembled in the clearing, and all the costumes were discarded and heaped in a pile. There was the Jester's hat, Compass's guns, Florence's lamp, and the kangaroo suit, amongst others, stacked high on top of each other, and right up there at the summit sat a very deflated pink cat.

It was great to be rid of their second skins, as the many stretches and twists testified and the cramps vanished. It was decided that everyone should split into small groups and go their own separate ways. Chester and Arabella teamed up with Compass, and the uninvited Mousellini tagged along as well. Lots of goodbyes and good lucks later, the mice all emerged from the dusty prison, their eyes squinted as the first light they had seen in a long time attacked them from every angle before they gradually adjusted to the scene before them. It was a beautiful sight: glorious sunshine, swaying trees, fresh air, and the birds of many colours, noisily singing.

# 7 Homeward Bound

"We will go this way!" Compass declared in a voice Victor would have been very proud of as he took control and led the way. Chester was only too willing to follow him, as Compass was apparently good with directions.

Many fields and dangerous roads were crossed in this new dangerous world, as the intrepid quartet quickly put distance between themselves and the now barely visible cheese factory and all its memories. The featureless landscape was now being negotiated at a great pace. It was a land once covered by the sea, which had left it so flat there were no hills or mountains to be seen. Cars rumbled by as Chester shielded Arrabella's eyes from the few unfortunate animals of the night who had not made it to the other side.

Three hours later, and after many a mile, Chester noticed a familiar sight and he called out to Compass, with a puzzled expression on his face, "I am sure we passed that sign about an hour ago." Arrabella and Mousellini agreed, as the fat chef sat down on a boulder to rest his aching feet.

"No, no, no, you are very much mistaken," came the reply from the know-it-all Compass, who strode purposefully onward shouting, "Follow me!" in an authoritative manner.

Night fell and the now disheveled group came to a long-awaited halt; they were very tired and ever so hungry. They could hear all manner of noises as they sat down and ate the many titbits the surrounding farmland yielded, and this field that they had stopped in had ample grain. The starving Mousellini stuffed himself, gathering a huge pile in front of him. It was a lovely change from just eating cheese over the past few years, he thought to himself as he smashed open yet another pea pod that he had found earlier.

The moon now shone brightly in the star-covered sky, illuminating the very place the exhausted group sat. They moved slightly backwards, under the cover of the dancing corn as the wind started to blow, and the hoot, hoot, hoot, of the all-seeing owl sent shivers down their spines and rooted them firmly to the new spot. A fine rain now began to fall and added to their woes; it would be a long night for the cold and wet travellers, as they were now too scared to sleep.

As the hours slowly passed, Chester began to tell them all about Anfield and the welcome that, if they decided to go there, awaited them. He may have slightly exaggerated some things but the tired trio agreed and decided that, in fact, that was where they should head for. They knew it would be a long and perilous journey, but it would be worth it in the end, Chester assured them. Chester finally got to sleep, just when it was time to get up. The sun had risen early and now shone brightly, and the ripe corn continued to sway rhythmically in the gentle wind.

Compass was raring to go. "Come on, Chester, let's go. No slackers here if you please!" he called out loudly, startling Chester who lay there in a daze. Compass waltzed off, not knowing where he was going, but giving the impression that he did. The weary Chester climbed to his feet and dragged his even wearier body slowly behind the front running Compass. He was really struggling to keep up, so Arrabella offered him some support, but pride made Chester politely decline her help, as he decided to make the extra effort. Five hours, two carrot fields and a potato crop later, Compass finally stopped. His fur was matted and encrusted with mud, his feet throbbed and he felt like crying, but he had to stand firm and prove himself to those who followed.

He turned to relay his orders like another Victor, but he needn't have bothered, his three co-travellers had already slumped to the ground, partially hidden amongst the leafy foliage. Sleep was not very far away. This time Chester slept really well, as the tiredness from this two-day journey had finally caught up with him. Nothing could disturb him as he dreamed pleasant thoughts. Arrabella huddled close to Chester, Mousellini even closer, but as the strong smell of cheese lingered in the air, Mousellini was told to huddle somewhere else.

Chester thought he could hear something, or rather someone shouting loudly. "Look-a at this, come and-a look-a ov-a here."

Chester had heard something, or rather someone as his long sleep was now broken and he began to stir. Mousellini had climbed a beanstalk in the neighbouring field and was surveying the land all around, whilst frantically waving and gesturing to everyone to join him and see what he had found.

"Come-a ov-a here, look-a at this," he continued, as Chester, Compass and Arrabella raced forward and started to scale the slippery stems.

Arrabella asked Mousellini as she climbed, "Is it a farm? Have you found a farm?"

"No," Mousellini replied in a now quieter voice as he was joined by his friends at the top of the crop. "I have-a nott-a found-a a farm-a," he continued, as he pointed to his left, "I have found-a that damned-a sign-a again!"

Chester angrily turned towards Compass just in time to see the timid mouse sliding down the beanstalk as fast as he could, as if it was a fireman's pole. Compass hid for a long time. The broad bean crop afforded him a good hiding place, but eventually as Chester's anger subsided Compass made his way back, ready to face any flak that awaited him.

"Sorry," Compass said quietly as he rejoined the group. "I thought I knew where I was going, but I obviously didn't. I can only hope you can accept my apologies," he stated meekly.

Chester had now mellowed as he approached his sullen friend and hugged him tightly, but he said quite firmly,

"I shall take the lead now. Is that okay?" Everyone breathed a sigh of relief and agreed that Chester was the best mouse for the job.

Arrabella expressed a wish to go over to the annoying sign. "It must say something … I am going to find out what."

Compass, head still slightly bowed, shouted out sarcastically after her,

"Of course, it will say something for that is what signs do. They say something, don't they." Chester gave Compass a steely stare and urged Arrabella to continue with her mission. It was quite apparent that everyone's nerves were being tested as tempers frayed. Arrabella had only been gone for a couple of minutes when she hurriedly returned.

Although breathless, she was still able to excitedly deliver her message. "It says the trans-pennine route, the Cheshire lines, and underneath there is an arrowed sign pointing to Liverpool. I think we are on the right track!" she enthusiastically proclaimed. At last a ray of hope lifted their spirits and another mass huddle and a bit of a cuddle between Arrabella and Chester ensued. There was a new-found urgency amongst them, and they could not wait to be on their way.

A hearty breakfast was eaten and their energy levels quickly rose, "READY?" Chester shouted.

"READY," came the reply, and away they went. The ground beneath them was very uneven and made travelling difficult, but this was only a minor inconvenience to them as their goal spurred them on. But there was no getting away from it. A long journey such as this one begins to take its toll, and as the early fast pace slowed, they all began to weaken. To make matters worse, black clouds began to assemble overhead and the wind picked up. They could ill afford another soaking, but that is what they would get if they didn't find cover and find it quickly. And as if by magic, that cover appeared.

Mousellini spotted it first and uttered in his Italian twang, "Look-a at this. See what a I havv-a found-a!" whilst excitedly jumping up and down and craning his neck trying to get a better look as a fallen branch obscured his view.

Not one other of the disheveled group registered much of an interest, but as Mousellini's antics became more exaggerated, Chester began to take notice, as he thought to himself, it had to be more than just another sign, and he asked the chef what it was. Mousellini pointed in the direction of the reason for all of his commotion, and although it was a distance away, he could tell it was a very large farm.

The fast pace that had become a very slow stroll was now a fast pace once again, as the rag-tag quartet summoned up energy they never knew they had and began to make light of the many stony obstacles in their path with a new-found vigour. Nothing would hinder their progress now, even as the first droplets of rain began to fall.

By the time the four thoroughly drenched mice had reached the farm, darkness had, once again, descended and cast its cloak over the broken buildings and rickety barns. Chester and company could hardly see more than a few feet as they waited in single file, pressed hard up against a wall. Chester tried to survey the scene as he peered around into the empty courtyard. He couldn't see anything, but he could feel the cold uncomfortable cobblestones beneath his feet. It reminded him of the Anfield alleyways. He paused and began to reflect once again. He thought of Giblet, and what he would have done in this situation, how would he have reacted. Chester considered all of his options at length as he studied the lie of the land further, for he had his friends' safety uppermost in his mind.

Compass began to push first, as he couldn't wait any longer to find some shelter as his wet fur now failed to keep him warm and he began to shiver. Chester told him firmly to behave himself, but it was all to no avail, for although he quite easily held back the skinny Compass, the fat Mousellini was just too much, as the combined weight of the two undisciplined mice thrust forward, knocking Chester out of the way. Arrabella saved Chester from his fall and gave him an affectionate look. She was really impressed by the composure he had shown, and a quick kiss told him so. "If only she had known me two weeks ago, she wouldn't have thought as much," Chester mused.

Chester and Arrabella chased after and caught up with the impulsive pair and once again, Chester led the way as he quickly resumed command. Large barns stood idle and broken, towering high above them, dwarfing these dwarves. Creaking resounded all around as the ill-fitting doors swung to and fro in the strong wind.

No one lived here anymore, but Chester knew from experience not to take anything for granted as he rushed across the threshold and into the shed to his left, beckoning everyone to follow. Good choice, Chester. Old haystacks stood tall reaching towards the breached and shattered roof, that still provided enough shelter for their needs. Grain that had seen better days spewed out from gnawed openings in tired sacks, filling all the crevices in the floor, and soon filling the emptiness in this group's empty bellies.

"It's so quiet here," Chester said.

"So peaceful," replied Arrabella.

"So calm," remarked Compass who added, as the tightly packed straw brought warmth to his body, "I could stay here forever." Mousellini just chomped on his grain, until his chomping gave way to snores, and as the wind and rain subsided, he slept like a baby for the first time in days and was quickly joined by the others as they, too, succumbed.

The rays of light that broke through the cracked barn provided the alarm call to wake them from their slumbers; the pleasant night had given way to an even pleasanter day.

# 8  Danger Overhead

It was now time for the fully rejuvenated and refreshed foursome to push on and continue with their long trek. All the grumbles and squabbles of the previous day were forgotten and the fragile friendships were now mended. The calm didn't last long, though. It couldn't, everything was going too well, as Mousellini walked out of the shed and took a few steps forward.

It wasn't heard but it was seen as it swooped silently and elegantly downwards from the sky. The last-second tuck of the wings as talons were made ready should have signalled the end of the Italian chef, but Chester, with the speed of light and quickness of thought, raced forward and with the strength of three mice, barged into his friend, sending him to the ground and out of the grasping clutches of the killer hawk. Mousellini lay on his back, and with his eyes facing the sky, caught his first glimpse of the flying attacker, and with the help of Chester, quickly regained his footing and ran back to the sanctuary of the shed and hoped for safety, as the hawk effortlessly repositioned itself and once again targeted its prey.

"*Run, run!*" Chester shouted.

"I am," gasped Mousellini, "I am."

"Faster then, faster," Chester demanded, as the whooshing sound of air parting closed in from behind. The fur stood up on the two mice's necks, as the frightening screech of the winged assassin echoed all around and immediately above its retreating meal. Eight legs on land proved better than two wings in flight as, at the last second, at the moment of truth, Chester and Mousellini reached the shelter of the bales of hay and disappeared within.

The hawk was foiled again as all thoughts of a tasty breakfast now turned to thoughts for his own safety, as he sped headlong towards the straw wall. He twisted and he turned and just managed to avoid a direct hit, but as he changed direction and surged upwards in a split-second flash, he collided with a section of the supportive beams. There was a tremendous thud that brought feathers cascading to the ground, wings fluttered slowly and then stopped, as the stunned hawk came to rest. He was trapped by his head in a V-shaped wedge, a place where one beam met another. The near-lifeless bird's frail body now hung, suspended high above, as his weak legs scratched at the rotten wood and then stopped.

Five minutes passed. It was enough time for Chester and Mousellini's trembling to have worn off. Arrabella peered into their hideaway and called to them to come out. The frightened duo emerged, albeit very, very slowly. Arrabella kissed Chester on top of his head, and saved one for Mousellini too, but she wished she hadn't, as she quickly recoiled when the taste and the smell of stale cheese that Mousellini could not rid himself of, exploded onto her lips. Chester looked up at the suspended bird and thought he could detect the slightest of quivers, as Arrabella began to usher him to the door, saying it was now time to go.

They all reached the door together and prepared to exit, but a slight groan and a moan brought Chester to a halt. The wounded hawk began to stir, his wings moved, and his still weak legs started to scratch at the wood again. The moans were getting louder. They were begging moans, the moans of someone in distress. Chester brought his front feet back inside from the outside and looked up once again at the tormented foe. He looked at Arrabella and announced in a soft voice, "We can't leave him like that … we must help him."

"Are you mad?" Compass shouted, or with words to that effect. "He will kill you and us. Leave him where he is and let's go now!" A bit of the old Chester resurfaced, and with a look that said he wasn't listening, he turned and paced towards the wooden struts. He took a deep breath and began to climb. Gone was the need to run and jump, as he had done with the slippery backyard door a few weeks ago. No, he scaled it effortlessly like a seasoned mountaineer and a few seconds later, reached the trapped bird. It was now that Chester could see the enormity of the large sharp beak that had threatened his life moments before; it now hung open, sucking in and desperately gulping the air as its tongue gently throbbed within. The wretched hawk's eyes moved irregularly from side to side. Chester didn't know if he was being watched, but he began to tentatively chew at the splintered beam. Arrabella did not know what to do either, "Shall I? Shan't I?" but then she did. Up she went and joined her man at the top, and she too began to gnaw, carefully avoiding the frightening jaws.

Chester and Arrabella nibbled nervously rather than enthusiastically at the decaying wood, each fully aware of the peril they were in, and wondering how they had managed to place themselves in such danger, but the sporadic moaning of the semi-conscious bird provided the answer, and spurred them on. A slight backward slip of the bird's body told them the wooden framework had begun to loosen its strong bonds. Both mice now broke off from their task just in time, as gravity took hold and dragged the poorly feathered beast back to ground.

There was no thud, only the slight rustle of breaking straw, as the heavy bird landed softly, and bounced twice on the large bale of hay below. And there he lay, moving and groaning but only just, as Chester and Arrabella descended again from the heights and rejoined Compass and Mousellini on solid ground.

"Now can we go?" Compass anxiously demanded to know, as he was in fear for his life. "You have done enough for him. You can't help him anymore. Let's go now!" he continued, almost pleading.

Chester glanced up at the prone feathered marauder lying face down above them on his compacted bed, and decided Compass was right. It was time to go and go quickly. Mousellini now checked the sky and checked it again. The whole experience had shattered his confidence, as his legs refused to move. Arrabella's gentle urgings and the sight of Compass racing across the cobbled courtyard, had the desired effect, as Mousellini's courage returned. Arrabella dragged Mousellini, and Mousellini dragged Arrabella. They nervously giggled as they ran with Chester out of the farm, and rejoined Compass on the nearby Cheshire lines.

They made a lot of progress that day, but might have made more if it hadn't been for the fact that they continued to look nervously behind, half expecting another frightening episode to befall them. Food was taken as they went, leaving half eaten peas and beans littering the trail behind them. And when they tired of the juicy carrots, an abundance of grain lay within easy access, and filled their stomachs.

The noisy singing of the swallows began to fade and disappear as the relied-upon nightfall began its approach, and signalled that maybe it was time for the four travellers to take a rest. Another night spent outside beckoned, but at least it was warm, and the tired band probably wouldn't notice anyway as they gave up the fight and easily went to sleep. Chester was the only one of the shattered four who had difficulty maintaining his sleep throughout the night. His new-found responsibilities weighed heavily on his mind, and his slumbers were continuously disturbed, as thoughts of further pitfalls refused to leave his brain and give him just a few hours of deserved peace. Well, that deserved peace didn't come, for as the morning arrived so did a mighty thump to the nose, and a heavy clump to Chester's head.

The same large hands that had hoisted him off the ground as he slid into the mound a week earlier now, once again, fitted neatly back into place, and lifted Chester high into the air. The red-capped Robarts's sneering and growling face came into view in Chester's right eye, but not his rapidly closing left. Violence was the name of the game for this red-suited thug, and he wasted no time in feverishly administering it. Victor could be heard loudly encouraging the continued assault, for he held Chester responsible for the destruction of his once great empire. Arrabella screamed and shouted, as did Mousellini and Compass, but their shouts were not the same as hers as they too took a fearful beating from Victor's army. Chester was not taking his punishment well. As he groveled around on the ground in the muck and the mud, he winced and groaned and gasped for breath, as Victor decided enough was enough and commanded Robarts to halt the relentless attack.

"I told you I wouldn't be so nice next time, didn't I?" Victor roared as he towered menacingly above, whilst looking down at the looking-up Chester at his feet. "You can count yourself lucky I have not let him finish the job!" Victor announced victoriously, whilst motioning towards the unfulfilled Robarts.

Chester's exhausted and injured body began to wilt further. He couldn't focus properly and he collapsed in a heap. He didn't feel the thud from the approaching ground, as his mind closed down in that instant.

"How did you find us?" the distraught and panic-stricken Arrabella demanded to know as her trickling tears now formed into a stream, and flowed down her face.

Victor bellowed out a mighty laugh before he triumphantly declared,

"Blame your fat friend, Mousellini. He stinks of cheese. We simply followed his scent." Victor's arrogance knew no bounds as he roared even louder. The bewildered Mousellini lifted his arms and smelt under his pits. He wondered what Victor was on about, as he couldn't smell any cheese.

Robarts protested loudly, and demanded he should be allowed the satisfaction of beating Chester to a pulp.

"I said no. Leave him be. He is no threat to us now. Do as I say and take hold of Arrabella," commanded Victor. He who had to be obeyed was quickly obeyed, but not until Robarts had delivered one last kick to Chester's side. The crumpled recipient did not respond, for he was already out for the count.

Robarts did as he was told and took hold of the struggling Arrabella. She did not make his task any easier, though, as she kicked out furiously in his direction. Her manicured claws that had since broken after days of rough travelling now struck home repeatedly, and would scar Robarts for a long time to come. It was hard to know who the captor was and who was the captive, as the little mouse lady with a wicked right hook proved more than a match for her cowering assailant; she continued to frustrate his every move. Victor, the always-sitting-on-the-sidelines-

Victor, decided at long last that he had to intervene, and as he moved forward ever so cautiously, trying to avoid the windmill arms of the feisty Bella, he pushed Robarts firmly in the back. sending him hurtling headlong into a measured fist. Victor seized his opportunity and sneakily managed to overpower and subdue the hysterical mouse, the one he had long held plans to marry. Arrabella, now tired and dirty, gave up the unequal struggle and allowed herself to be hauled unceremoniously back to her feet. Robarts was very, very angry and his rough handling went unnoticed by the weak Victor, who began to cry as he bent down to pick up his treasured sword. The long rapier blade was no longer straight, and it now pointed north, south, east and west.

Victor was mad and Victor was angry as he jumped up and down trying to realign his trusty cutlass. His mood wasn't helped though, as one of his underlings suggested "Maybe you could use it to fight around corners!"

Victor turned quickly and furiously demanded to know who had said that, whilst delivering the most unnerving of scowls, and a growl guaranteed to send shivers down his subordinates' spines, and it did, as his demand was now met with all of his soldier mice frantically pointing and accusing one another. All hell was about to break loose, but it wasn't the hell that was expected, as a *Whoosh* and a *Swoosh* interrupted and invaded the scene. In an instant, so unbelievably quick, Victor and Robarts left this earth as two mighty claws buried themselves deep into the red uniforms and tightened their grip. There was no escape and there was no time for screams as they disappeared high into the sky, soaring towards the clouds with the bird Chester and Arrabella had saved only a few hours before. Arrabella, Compass and Mousellini didn't move. They couldn't. This shocking and unexpected encounter rooted them firmly to the spot, but that didn't stop Victor's army as they ran this way and that in every direction, fleeing for their lives. Everything in that moment was saturated in a deathly silence, nothing moved. No birds sang and no wind blew. Time seemed to stand still. Chester suddenly sat up and let out a feeble moan as his injuries hurt but his senses were slowly returning. His supportive friends all rushed quickly to his side, and tenderly dragged him under cover from the burning sunlight.

Everyone rather excitedly and all at once tried to explain what had just happened. No one could believe it, but it was true. The hawk they had rescued had returned the favour.

"You couldn't make it up even if you tried!" Compass announced with great wisdom.

Arrabella gently tended to Chester's wounds. He winced like a baby as she slightly touched his bruised torso, remarking "You're still handsome Chester, even with one eye closed."

This new and eventful day now became a day to rest, as Chester was in no fit state to travel. He lay on a bed of uncomfortable stalks, but he didn't care as he had the beautiful Arrabella at his side.

A light rain fell for barely an hour, but it was just enough time for Arrabella to moisten Chester's grazes and lower his temperature. As the day wore on, Chester felt a whole lot better, and apart from the odd ache he was beginning to feel as good as new. He drifted in and out of sleep for the rest of the afternoon and through the early evening as the sun set. Twilight time came and twilight time went as Chester snoozed on and on. Night time passed, but he didn't notice, and as the early dawn arrived with the constant chattering of the birds, Chester woke and sprang to his feet, energised and raring to go.

"Nosh-a slow flast," Mousellini spluttered as a mouthful of breakfast received a crunch from his powerful molars.

Chester, not understanding what his friend had just said, asked rather bemusedly,

"What is all that nonsense you're uttering, Mousellini?"

Mousellini swallowed hard and cleared his throat. He looked at Chester, slightly angered because his meal was being interrupted and he repeated, "I said-a, nott-a so fast, do you nott-a understand-a the Eenglish?" His eyes drifted towards his forehead as he muttered a final "Mamma-mia!" and then continued with his food.

Suddenly the *Whoosh* but this time without the *Swoosh* returned. Everyone's eyes quickly scanned all around as heads turned this way and that. The friendly hawk of yesterday had returned and now stood aloft, proudly perched on a post. Chester urged everybody to be very quiet, and not to show themselves as they edged closer back inside and under the cover of the towering plants. They didn't know what to expect as they were unsure of the bird's intentions.

Unbeknown to Chester's brigade, the hawk had already spotted them and rasped out a bit of a greeting:

> Come out, my friends, and don't be afraid,
>
> I can see you with my eyes as you hide in the shade.
>
> Come out and join me, for there's no need for alarm,
>
> My intentions are honourable, I mean you no harm.
>
> I hung from the rafters helpless and dazed,
>
> You saved my life and deserve to be praised.
>
> I offer my thanks and I shall never forget,
>
> I will repay your kindness as I am forever in your debt.

Well, Chester was taken aback by this, and very surprised, for he was expecting something much worse than a frightening bird breaking into verse. Chester, Mousellini, Arrabella, and Compass now had a very big decision to make, a possibly life-threatening decision. Arrabella said,

"Let's go out," in a very quiet voice. She felt the hawk was genuine. "He could have taken any one of us, but he didn't, he took Robarts and Victor. We can trust him," she now insisted more determinedly. Chester agreed, as did the other two, and all together they walked slowly out from their hideaway and took up the bird's invitation.

"He...he...he...hello," Compass nervously half-murmured, as he reluctantly looked up and stared his possible executioner in the face. "Wha...wh...wh... what is your name, please, sir?" the completely petrified Compass asked as his eyes were averted from the green-eyed gaze that the hawk returned.

The huge bird could sense Compass's unease and began to speak.


Relax little mouse, I mean what I say,

I come in peace, I'm not looking for prey.

I have eaten many a mouse in the past,

But this day, my friend, will not be your last.

I meant what I said – an honest heart beats within,

And I will answer your question my name is PEREGRINE.

Chester decided to take a chance, and dispensed with all of his inhibitions, and called up to Peregrine to join them down on the ground, for he felt that they had all been out in the open and exposed long enough for the hawk to have attacked and he hadn't.

Peregrine floated down from off his perch and effortlessly and silently joined the now fearless group below. It was now that the full enormity of this majestic bird hit home, as he slowly approached in bounds rather than a walk. His huge powerful wings, that stretched for what seemed like miles to the small mice, aided Peregrine with his balance. Many colours adorned the shiny plumage and contrasted markedly from the huge black beak, and his long yellow legs housed the large sharp weapons of destruction.

Chester, Arrabella, and the others, now feeling a little bit more comfortable in Peregrine's company, embarked eagerly asking all manner of questions of their new feathered friend. He willingly answered every one of their enquiries with a natty line in poetry, but stopped short of giving any details when pressed to reveal what had happened to Victor and Robarts. No, he only met their searching questions, with his snake-like tongue whipping out, and washing over the menacing beak, whilst stating, "You won't be having any more trouble from them."

Peregrine wanted to know all about the small band's situation, and Chester wasted no time at all in telling him of their plight, and how they were travelling to Anfield, but it was proving very difficult as well as really dangerous. Peregrine listened intently to his every word. Chester told him about all the things that had happened to him in quick succession in his very short life, Peregrine found it really difficult to laugh, what with his beak and all, but he was most definitely amused, but not Arrabella, Compass, and Mousellini. They were more amazed than amused that this mouse who was now a tower of strength to them, someone they had come to rely on so much, could have been such a buffoon just a few short weeks ago.

When all the amusement from Peregrine and the amazement from his new friends had died down, Peregrine suddenly, after a little thought, announced, "Maybe I can help you in your quest."

"How?" Arrabella excitedly exclaimed in a squeaky type of voice, imploring Peregrine to continue.

Peregrine wasn't immediately forthcoming with his answer, as he stood there quietly, and pondered, and mused, and even deliberated. He put the final touches to his hastily thought-out plan and presented it to another part of his brain for final ratification.

"I shall air-lift you to Maghull!" he gleefully announced, as he proudly puffed his chest out and continued, "That's as far as I can take you, as I do not want to encroach on another hawk's patch. What do you think?" He squawked out loudly, feeling really chuffed with himself.

Mousellini and company now all looked towards each other, their eyes mutually expressed the same feelings, and without any discussion, they all together and all at once shouted out deliriously, "Yes, yes, please, Peregrine. Thank you so much!" without fully realising the enormity of what this journey would involve. Chester jumped up and down on the spot, and waved his arms high above his head like a crazy mouse, until he noticed Arrabella's wide-eyed surprise at his wild antics, which brought him to his senses.

He suddenly stopped his shenanigans and let out a little cough before he asked Peregrine in a now sensible voice, "When do you think we could go?"

Peregrine replied immediately and loudly with an enthusiastic tone, "Let's go now, for there is no time like the present. It won't take me long as I know the route off by heart. Fifteen minutes maximum, that's all it will take me to get you there. How about it?" he eagerly continued, feeling even more pleased with himself.

The next ten minutes were spent putting the final details of the plan into some sort of context. There were a lot of, what ifs, and what abouts, if this or that should happen, that type of query, until eventually every scenario had been thoroughly examined, explained, and understood by them all, and they were ready to go. Mousellini lined up next to Compass, and Arrabella stood alongside Chester, ready for departure. Peregrine took to the air and prepared his gracefully flapping wings in flight. He returned moments later and began to hover, almost motionlessly, as he adjusted his position inches above the orderly foursome's heads. Ever so slowly, the huge talons closed in and around Chester's and Arrabella's bodies. They fitted snugly like a harness, as the mice began to fumble about, trying to get a secure hold. Compass and Mousellini were doing exactly the same on the other leg. Peregrine called out to his passengers like the pilot of a plane, and asked if they were all ready: "Yes!" came the excited but also nervous reply, as they settled back and gripped the shiny black claws tightly and held on for dear life. There would be no in-flight service on this journey, as Peregrine made ready for departure.

Suddenly they were off as wings flapped rhythmically together and produced some lift, quickly putting distance between the bird and earth. The ground disappeared from sight, as all the mice now tightly closed their eyes. Everything was and then everything wasn't going to plan, as the lopsided Peregrine announced he was returning to base. The unequal weight below was making him lurch to his left-hand side, forcing him to go around in a circle. Chester reluctantly swapped places with Compass, and then swapped back again, as they tried repeatedly and confusingly to work out how to distribute the cargo a bit more evenly. It was just as well that the smart Peregrine was on hand to referee the shambles beneath him, and dictate that it might be better if the fat Mousellini had a leg to himself. Compass joined Chester and Arrabella in their carriage and just about managed to squeeze into the middle of them, separating and frustrating the passionate pair, but he didn't care.

"Are we ready?"

"Yes, we are!" came the collective cries all around, as, once again, lift-off was achieved.

*Whoosh, swoosh, whoosh, swoosh,* and then "Urghh," were the sounds breaking out from everywhere and everyone as Peregrine scaled the heights and the reluctant passengers experienced G force. The wind that was non-existent down below now challenged them from every angle, and the mice all struggled to catch their breath, as teeth chattered within stretched cheeks. Peregrine couldn't hear the screams and squeals or feel their nausea, as he soared higher and higher, higher than a hawk would normally fly, but he didn't want to be spotted by any of his friends, because if he was, he would never live it down; for a hawk not eating a mouse was unheard of.

They must have been the longest fifteen minutes ever, but eventually they were over as Maghull loomed into view. Peregrine began to hover once more and then started to slowly descend to earth, as his fantastic eyesight identified a suitable landing zone.

"Is everyone okay?" Peregrine sheepishly asked, for he probably knew his furry friends would be feeling rather the worse for wear, and they were, as he glided in for touchdown. Arrabella was the first to run into the bushes that ran alongside the towpath of the Leeds to Liverpool canal, as it wasn't very lady-like to vomit in front of all of these onlookers. Mousellini followed closely behind, as his breakfast began to make an appearance. Peregrine stood there. His face feigned fake surprise as he refused to acknowledge Chester's prolonged look of disdain. Peregrine, feeling the need to focus all the negative attention away from himself, pointed with his outstretched left wing in a southerly direction, outlining to Chester that if they followed this long and undulating trail, they would eventually reach Liverpool and home.

Arrabella and Mousellini, still feeling very poorly but considerably lighter, emerged from the bushes and joined Chester and Compass in thanking Peregrine for everything he had done for them, and impressing upon him that they would never forget. Many moist eyes were the last thing Peregrine saw as he suddenly took to the air. Heads turned this way and that as the mighty bird performed a bit of a fly-by with military precision, and above all took in the cheering and the waving, and the many shouts of farewell aimed in his direction. Peregrine returned the sentiments as he called back and left one last ditty.

Goodbye my friends, for that is what you are.

I will remember you always as I fly near and afar.

You've changed my life from the moment we met.

From this day forward, to mice I am no longer a threat.

I mean that sincerely, I can promise you that;

Mouse is now off my menu, I will make do with a rat.


Everyone cheered, but Peregrine didn't hear them for he was now gone, as a dark grey cloud appeared, engulfing him in an instant. A light rain began to fall, causing the sombre quartet to run for cover and deal with their emotions elsewhere. They all decided maybe it would be best if they slept for the rest of the day, and Mousellini decided not to eat for the rest of the day as well, as he collapsed into a nearby bush with his upset stomach.

## 9  Ship Ahoy

A huge storm blew up and lasted the entire night. The bushes were providing little or no cover at all, but an empty packet of cheese and onion crisps came to the rescue of the soaked mice, and the bedraggled quartet climbed in. Mousellini felt really comfortable and at home in the rustling bag, but the strong smell of cheese just brought bad memories flooding back for the other three. Flooding probably wasn't the right word to use, as the now torrential rain was unrelenting, quickly building up ferocious streams that flowed rapidly by.

It was a very tight squeeze in the polythene tent and it was making for a very restless night, as the thunderous rain that repeatedly struck it echoed long and hard. Compass was ejected at least three times in the first hour in their new home, as he continuously, but unsuccessfully, tried to squeeze in between Chester and the lovely

Arrabella once more. Eventually and rather reluctantly, he had to accept that a position snuggled up next to Mousellini was his only option. He tossed and he turned for what seemed like an eternity as the pungent aroma persisted, from which only sleep would bring him some relief.

The strong wind continued to batter them for hours to come, trying to suck their sleeping bag high into the air, but the combined weight of the now comatose mice held the bag firm and just about kept them rooted to the ground. It was now that Chester, Compass, and Arrabella gave thanks that the oversized Mousellini was still around.

The warmth of the tightly-compacted bodies had done its job, for as they awoke from their slumbers, totally refreshed, their fur was now bone dry. The scene that greeted them as they climbed out from under the plastic duvet was not very inviting at all. The towpath landing strip of yesterday was now submerged under a sticky black sea of mud, carpeting the trail for as far as the eye could see.

Chester put his left leg forward to test the depth of the slurping black mass, and it quickly disappeared, as he would have done also if he hadn't shown such caution. Chester now reasoned that with the trail now being seemingly impassable, maybe it would be unwise to travel that day, and Arrabella and Compass wholeheartedly agreed. But the angry protests from the starving Mousellini, whose settled stomach now demanded food, implored them to overturn their decision. Mousellini's aggressive ranting was met with a steely determination from Chester, who emphatically declared, "We are staying here until it all dries out. You go if you want to, as it's far too dangerous for any of us to leave." Mousellini cut short his protestations as he was taken aback that his word meant nothing to his fellow travellers, and he furiously barked out his retort,

"Okay-a, I will-a. I'll-a see-a you all-a late-a, so there-a. Good-a bye-a." And with that, and without much thought to his strategy, he strode forward and instantly plunged headlong into the gooey bath and disappeared from sight.

Chester, Arrabella, and Compass all rushed forward to help their stricken comrade, but all their fears quickly turned to laughter as the now blackened Mousellini righted himself and emerged at the surface. The spluttering mud-lark urged them to stop their hysterics as he spat out a mouthful of sludge and screamed for help. It was really difficult for them as they tried to pull the overweight mouse out of the gluey pool that didn't want to let him go, whilst laughing their heads off. Slowly but surely, the exertions of the three mice paid off and the encrusted Mousellini clambered out and back onto terra firma.

Another light rain began to fall and that settled any arguments. As Arrabella, Chester, and Compass retreated into the bag, Mousellini took advantage of this natural shower as he stayed put, allowing the clinging mud to be washed away. Arrabella proved she would make a good mother one day as she called out loudly with a devilish grin, "And don't forget to wash behind your ears!" Everyone fell about laughing once more, and so did Mousellini, as the temperamental Italian sought to repair his fractured friendships.

"Is there no end to this miserable weather?" Compass complained over and over again, as the rain continued to frustrate the downcast four throughout the day. All they could do was to lie there and watch as the world went by. Mother Duck noisily swam past, her brood following closely behind. Mother Duck returned and again swam noisily past. Compass reckoned she was doing it on purpose, trying to agitate an already agitated mouse. The grey heron with its long beak slowly flew by, just about skimming the surface looking for its next meal. His beady eye seemed to train on Chester and his chums. A few moments later he returned and now his other beady eye investigated the scene, as all the mice slowly retreated a little further back inside their waterproof pouch. The grey heron must have, at this point, accepted that there must be a crisp packet with four heads and continued with his flight.

It wasn't planned, but everyone took it in turns to sleep. It was proving incredibly tiring just lying there without anything to do. Nothing disturbed their inactivity apart from the periodic rumblings from Mousellini's empty belly.

Nightfall approached and the moon began to make its appearance. The thoroughly dejected mice wondered if they would ever finish this journey, and each conversation they started seemed to end in an argument, as they constantly bickered. Suddenly, out of the darkness the tremendous roar of an engine, similar to that in Les S. Shocks's van, interrupted the silence, and brought the four mouse heads to attention. The still waters of a few moments before began to part as a bow sliced through them like a pair of scissors. The same waters churned and bubbled as the whirling propeller propelled the *Liverpool Belle* into sight.

A strong light illuminated the old wooden boat that was bedecked with a million flower pots, as it moved in closer to the canal's side. The compressing water sloshed and splurged as the former barge came to rest alongside and directly opposite eight unseen eyes. Two ropes instantly flew through the air and landed almost silently on the bank, cushioned by the thick mud. One rope waited forward to be tied and one waited aft, as a portly man with a white cap covered in gold braid, jumped ashore with a confident air. He didn't remove his pipe from his mouth as he managed to shout out loudly, "That will do, my dear, turn her off!" As the Belle was now safely moored.

Henry Smith had sailed these waters every weekend for the past seven years. It had been his favourite pastime, and now it was his life, as he now lived on the *Liverpool*

*Belle* full time with his wife, Aggy, ever since he had retired from his job as a lollipop man outside the Bootle Strand six months previously. Aggy loved this life as much as her husband. Even though this was only the canal, she reckoned the sea was in her blood, as her grandfather was a merchant seaman during the First World War.

Henry Smith settled down at the table, ready for the meal Aggy had been lovingly preparing for ages. The light that now drenched the gently swaying vessel visibly highlighted to the watching mice the large fork, full of potatoes, heading towards Henry's lips. The doting Aggy grunted out a quiet "Ahem" and suggested it might be better if Henry removed his pipe first. Each fork-load that ferried the potato, carrot and beef from the plate to Henry's palate was meticulously scrutinised by the hungry four, especially Mousellini. The steaming sticky toffee pudding with lashings of custard added to his torment, so he buried his head in his hands and pretended he was imagining things, but a running commentary from the other three proved too much, especially when the cheese board arrived. He couldn't stop himself now, as he jumped out from his synthetic shelter and ran quickly forward and once again plunged headlong into the forgotten mud. Once more Compass and co. had to come to their absent-minded friend's rescue, pulling, and shoving, and heaving as a tug-of-war ensued between the three mice and the grasping bog. The angry Mousellini clambered out muttering all sorts of not-so-nice words. His intention was to immediately suppress any forthcoming laughter heading his way, but he needn't have bothered. Chester, Arrabella, and Compass were beyond laughing as they too muttered, "Stupid fool".

The unrelenting rain had now relented and there was nowhere for Mousellini to take a shower. The heavy mud held firm as he groped and licked at his sagging fur in a forlorn attempt to smarten himself up. Henry Smith rose from the table. He was fully sated after such a lovely meal. "Shall we leave the dishes till later, my dear?" he enquired as he picked up his smoker and loaded the tobacco.

"I think you are probably right," the now tired Aggy replied, as she took hold of Henry's pipe and had a quick puff. Aggy extinguished the light in the kitchen, and followed her husband in retiring to another part of the vessel with knitting pattern in hand. Her long and enjoyable day was almost at an end.

Four mouse silhouettes disappeared along with the vanishing light, and everything was now very quiet and still. The cold and the damp and hunger were now all starting to take their toll on Mousellini as he began to shiver uncontrollably, as his exposure to the elements was beginning to weaken his resolve. Chester eyed the braided ropes that tightened and slackened in equal measure as the *Liverpool Belle* drifted in and out with the gentle movements of the murky waters.

"We could scale those ropes and climb aboard," he announced unexpectedly, startling Compass and the others as they wearily slumped back into the bag, for they had already resigned themselves to another night out in the open. Compass joined Chester at the foot of the tied-up lash, his eyes bulging with excitement as he quickly realised Chester's plan had a chance.

"Over here, over here!" Compass shouted out, as he urged Arrabella and Mousellini to come and see. Arrabella complied and did what she was told, but only because she wanted to find out what was the cause of Compass's childlike exuberance. Mousellini wasn't so fast, though, as the heavy mud slowed his advance.

"Look..." Chester said, as he began to explain his calculated assumption that "...if we time it just right, and begin to climb as the boat drifts from the bank and the ropes tighten, we could be aboard and warm in no time at all."

"Excellent … not a problem … easy peasy." were some of the more toned- down eager comments as euphoria spread amongst them all, and they all agreed that this shouldn't be a problem for four fleet-footed mice.

The boat began its drift and up they went, Compass first. His feet hardly touched the tightly-interwoven rope as he bounded quickly up and reached the top. Chester and Arrabella followed his lead in an instant. Their balance was perfect as they joined Compass high above, and asked for "Permission to come aboard, sir?" Mousellini, the well-rounded Mousellini, unhealthy and unkempt, with feet full of mud, took his first wobbly steps, with his even more wobbly belly pressed hard against the slender rope. He was bereft of all finesse and confidence as he held on dearly, unable to move. And then as the boat returned slowly inwards and the tough chords slackened, he nearly lost his footing and also his life, as cries of "Oh no!" and "No,

No!" and "Now, now!" From his encouraging friends baffled him all the more.

Mousellini would never make it as a trapeze artist, but as the rope began to straighten once more, he slowly started to inch his way forward. There was an absence of any skill involved as he edged closer to the top. Arrabella had long since closed her eyes, as Chester and Compass held out their hands and helped to haul him in. Arrabella ordered the mud-spattered chef to take a shower under the dripping tap before he would be allowed to join them at the table. Aggy had prepared far too much food, but she could rest assured that none of it would go to waste, as the hungry mice started its demolition. There was nothing orderly in their approach as they ravenously began to devour the sumptuous left overs. Table manners were non-existent as Mousellini ploughed in head first, just as he had done with the mud, straight into the sticky toffee pudding. Chester was no more laid back, and Compass greedily continued the trend; only Arrabella showed any restraint, because, after all, she was a lady.

Chester consumed the last of the carrots and had a munch on the spud. He didn't much fancy the beef, so he gave it a miss. Compass found out that he loved celery, as he danced all over the fresh salad. It was delicious but there wasn't enough. He decided he now needed something sweet to eat, so he climbed down out of the salad bowl and joined Mousellini at the pud, or rather in it, before the obese chef had polished it all off. He could not walk across the gooey plate. It was more of a wade, as the sickly sticky toffee clung to his fur, bringing him to a halt. A small black pellet that he thought was a piece of sponge caught his eye, and he quickly gathered it up in his paws and began to chew. Why had he not used his trusty senses though, he thought to himself, as he suddenly spluttered and ejected a piece of Mousellini's mud.

The light that invaded the long narrow kitchen as the switch was flicked, took the gluttonous diners by surprise. Not one of them moved as water fired ferociously out of the single tap and dishes began their dunk under soapy suds. Suddenly all hell broke out as hysterical screams rang out all around. They were terrible high-pitched squeals, very hard on the ears, as the frightened perpetrator dropped a plate, and leapt onto a chair shouting, *"MICE, MICE, MICE!"* as loudly as possible.

Aggy quickly dropped her needles and watched in horror as all of her new crocheting fell to the floor. She bounded into the kitchen to find her blubbering husband shaking uncontrollably, teetering on top of the stool. Her rock, her tower of strength was now a quivering wreck. Aggy did her best to calm Henry, as she sat him down and caressed the back of his neck to soothe his shattered nerves, and between his sobs, she managed to get a clearer picture about his long-held fear of mice, as his story unfolded.

Aggy, brush in hand, left her now reassured hubby in the living room and locked the door. The great mouse hunt was now on. As she clambered down the stairs and into the bowels of the boat, tiny sticky toffee footprints led the way. This mild-mannered lady, who liked nothing better than to knit one pearl one, now viciously brandished the brush high above her head and shouted out loudly as she tentatively peered into every nook and cranny, and savagely poked about under the mountings of the powerful engine.

Chester urged his fellow-hunted not to move, as he remembered this tactic had served him well during his many run-ins with the lady in Anfield with the bleach blond hair with the black stripe down the centre. Aggy continued her search for a good hour. She knew the mice were there but realised she would need more than just a brush, so she decided to leave them for now, but firmly locked the door behind her to prevent any escape. A few minutes later she returned and set six traps, smaller than the one Chester had witnessed in the yard in Anfield, but traps all the same. The door slammed shut once more as the little old lady donned her sweet exterior and rejoined her husband above.

Aggy decided to make a nice strong cup of tea for Henry and herself. She put an extra lump of sugar in his, as apparently, it would help him with the shock he had just suffered.

"Here you are, love," she said in a quiet consoling voice as she handed him the mug, "and a nice chocolate biscuit to go with it."

"You don't think any less of me do you, Aggy?" he meekly asked whilst averting his gaze from his wife. "I don't know what came over me. I thought I had overcome my childhood fear of mice." Aggy's reply came quickly as she reassured her husband of over thirty years' standing that he hadn't gone down in her estimation, but Henry wasn't so convinced as Aggy casually threw her knitting pattern towards him, and put his gold braided cap on her head.

Chester and company enjoyed a really good night's sleep, so different from the night before. The heat from the engine kept them warm for hours, and the sand in the fire bucket made for a comfortable bed.

Henry had eaten his breakfast in total silence, still embarrassed by the frailties he had shown the night before. Aggy, with a wicked sense of humour, could feel his unease, and allowed normality to return by placing Henry's cap back on his head where it rightfully belonged. A huge smile broke out across his face and he rose quickly, puffed out his chest and gave Aggy a big kiss.

"Shall we go, dear? Shall I untie the ropes?" he said, imploring his wife to agree, as he assumed the dominant role.

"Don't you normally start the engines, dear, and I untie the ropes?" Aggy insisted in a mischievous tone.

"Not today, dear. It's about time you played a more active part in the running of the boat, and I think you could maybe steer her sometime today," Henry stated as he jumped ashore. Aggy shook her head and picked up her broom, unlocked the door to the engine room and went on the prowl. The traps yielded nothing, and she began to wonder if the mice had managed to thwart her and make their escape. Aggy checked the oil, topped up the water, opened up the clutch, and pressed the ignition like a seasoned engineer. Henry had maintained his boat to the highest standards as the huge machine energised and roared into life. Aggy retreated quickly up the steps as the loud heartbeat of the vessel was all too much for her, but before she went outside, she allowed her eyes to sweep one last time around the buzzing room, searching for the elusive vermin. She still couldn't see them, for they had hidden well. Nevertheless, she closed the door firmly behind her.

Henry released the ropes and jumped back on board, as his dutiful wife took to the helm and gently steered the *Liverpool Belle* away from the muddy banks. The water began to churn violently as she pushed the accelerator fully to its hilt.

"Not so fast, my dear," Henry quietly ordered, not wanting to cause any upset, but already regretting allowing Aggy to take a more active role, as he thought his own position would be undermined.

The *Liverpool Belle* steadied at five miles per hour, effortlessly gliding as mile after mile slowly passed. The wind gently blew through Aggy's hair and Henry sucked in the untainted air.

"It is all so beautiful in this part of the country," Henry quietly muttered, as he observed the pleasant scene before him. Mother ducks quacked incessantly as they rode the bow wave, with numerous chicks following in their wake. Angry geese honked as their sunbathing along the banks was disturbed by the *Belle*'s powerful motor. Only a slice of bread hastily tossed towards them would pacify their scorn. Mighty oaks stood tall and the numerous weeping willows hung down over the water, heavily adorned with silky-haired pods, ready for dispersal. A huge five-storey, red-bricked building with windows boarded up came into view. This mill that had provided work for many a barge in years gone by now stood idle as it slowly aged. Its listed status was the only thing saving it from the bulldozer, but Henry couldn't decide if he agreed with this or not.

This idyllic scene above was not mirrored below. Mousellini, Chester, Arrabella and Compass were suffering intolerable pain, as the booming clanking engine relentlessly emitted its thunderous growls. The bewildered and frightened mice all covered their ears in a forlorn attempt to drown out the noise, but they were unsuccessful as the torture persisted. Mousellini began to gnaw at the old wood on the inside of the boat, and as his worrying quickly gathered pace, it seemed that this chewing provided some kind of comfort to him. Arrabella started to cry uncontrollably so Chester put his arms around her trying to console her, but he quickly removed them and once again protected his own ears, for a choice between gallantry and deafness was no choice at all.

Percy Jones called down to Henry from his vantage point on the bridge high above, as the *Liverpool Belle* slowly passed by underneath. His welcoming greetings signalled the arrival of the *Belle* back home once more in Bootle. Another one hundred yards or so and she would be at journey's end. Aggy waved up to Percy, who now returned to the job that Henry had vacated six months previously and stepped out into the busy traffic on Stanley Road, Bootle, not realising that he had left his lollipop stick still leaning against the bridge. The number 92 bus pulled up sharply with a penetrating screech of the brakes, and the smell of burning rubber hung in the air. The driver blasted his horn instinctively as he narrowly avoided hitting Percy full on, but a black taxi wasn't quite so lucky as it ploughed into a passing police car with its siren blaring loudly. Percy stood there trembling, unable to move as the irate drivers began to fight one another. A little girl, her hair in pigtails, put down her satchel and instigated the rescue of this veteran of many a school crossing, as she took the quivering Percy by the hand and led him back to the pavement and safety and his pole.

Mousellini's gnawing had become increasingly frantic. His constant nibbling continued to afford him some relief from the never-ending, monotonous thumping and drumbeat of the engine within. It was only a trickle at first, and actually it provided Mousellini with a bit of a drink, but suddenly a spluttering squirt developed and caught him full in the eye forcing him to recoil so as to avoid another direct hit. The trickle that had become a spluttering squirt suddenly became a gush as the old wood caved in with a mighty creak and a loud crack. The small hole was now a large gash, and water poured in, consuming the room in no time at all, and forcing the mice to swim for dear life. Bubbling steam rose high and the rising flood even higher as it swallowed and then silenced the hissing engine … forever.

Henry Smith lost his balance in the ensuing chaos, as the *Liverpool Belle* suddenly lurched to its left, sending poor Aggy overboard with a huge splash; Henry's pipe followed suit and quickly sank into the deep. Pots and pans crashed to the floor as deafening noises from a ship in distress resounded all around. Henry was struggling to regain his footing as he grovelled around on the slippery deck searching for a hold and his pipe, as the severe tilt continued unabated. Percy Jones and the little girl now gawped in horror as they witnessed the demise of the *Liverpool Belle*, a fine vessel for over thirty years as it slowly overturned in six feet of water and was now no more. The shocked and tearful captain couldn't believe what was happening, but happening it was as he reluctantly ejected himself from his boat and plunged into the murky waters and then went to the aid of his panic-stricken wife.

Aggy's arms flailed wildly and she more than once dealt Henry a glancing blow, but he eventually managed to subdue her and was able to drag her safely to the bank, and as he climbed out onto dry land, spitting out diesel and weed, he caught a last glimpse of his gold braided cap slowly floating past … with four sodden mice aboard.

## 10 A Rational Rat

All the mice now gathered their thoughts and their breath as the troubled, unsettled waters quickly ferried them back underneath the Bootle bridge. Their mystified gazes drifted away from the half submerged-wreck, and were now concentrated on the tremendous melée that ensued high above. The taxi driver hit a police man and the bus driver joined in. What could have been the cause of all this mayhem, the bewildered Mousellini wondered, as they distanced themselves from it all on the slow current.

Thirty minutes later, with Bootle now just a memory, the gold braided cap was itself now beginning to sink. It absorbed the water at a phenomenal rate forcing the frightened mice to act fast, and so Chester gave that time-honoured shout, as he assumed command and directed everyone to "Abandon ship!" Now mice can swim if they have too, and they certainly had to here, as the cap was overcome and spiralled out of sight as it sank into the deep. Chester reached the bank first and gave huge thanks that there just happened to be a large branch wedged tight against the canal's sides. He dragged himself on and went up and out, with his three companions in close attendance.

This fine summer's day could only get better or worse, and it did, for as they all had a collective shake, freeing themselves of the grimy water, they failed to notice they were now surrounded by five RATTUS NOVEGICUS, more commonly known as the brown rat. Chester immediately began to tremble as he stood there in a puddle of his own making, that now wasn't all water. Arrabella did what she did best and started to cry; Mousellini quivered and squealed, and Compass, well, he just fainted.

The five large rats closed in, in an ever-decreasing circle, but they didn't attack. It was as if they had received a warning or a signal not to, but if that was the case,

Chester hadn't heard it. The sworn enemies of many a mouse reared up onto their hind legs. They were a menacing sight but still they didn't press home their advantage. Chester now realised why he was still on this earth as he instantly recognised the even larger rat that pushed through the tightly packed huddle, a white blaze adorning his huge head. It was Flash or whatever his name was, from the yard back in Anfield.

Flash stood there and repeated the stare that had scared the living daylights out of Chester once before. It was left to Chester to say something, so he sheepishly said, "Hello," half expecting a bite at any moment. Flash moved forward once more, and then to everyone's surprise gave Chester a loving hug. Every mouse gasped and there were many sighs of relief as well, but not from Flash's friends, who all registered their amazement as they put their teeth away.

"I have thought about you every day," Flash quietly announced as he put Chester down. "You saved my life and I never thanked you, I should have but I didn't. I owe you a lot." This speech sounded very much like Peregrine's sentiments, but Chester wasn't complaining as he cockily replied, "Oh, it was nothing. Anyone would have done the same in my position." But he honestly couldn't remember what it was, this great deed he had done.

The rats were great company, not at all like they had been depicted in many a story. They put on a fine feast for their smaller cousins, and eventually this gathering developed into a wild party. Chester, in those moments, could see what life could and should be like with everyone coming together in friendship, no animosity shown, laughter and love in abundance. He sat down next to Flash and began to reflect once more on his short life and his shortcomings. He thought about the love of his mother, the friendship of Giblet, and how one good turn shown towards someone else can reap great benefits as that act can be repaid thrice over, as the Peregrine episode had done and now this situation with Flash.

Chester summoned Flash to move a little closer and whispered in his ear as the noisy din continued all around. He began to explain that he couldn't honestly remember saving him on purpose. It was just by chance that he had hiccupped at that time, causing the surprised rat to jump out of harm's way and thus avoid the peanut-buttered killer trap.

Flash pulled away slightly, and his body began to stiffen and shake. His eyes bulged and he bared his teeth, whilst giving Chester a stare that Chester didn't like. Chester braced himself and wondered what it was he had done wrong. Flash moved closer to Chester once more, and now it was his turn to whisper in the terrified mouse's ear, as he calmly said, "Well, I don't know whether I should eat you now as you are here under false pretences." Chester froze and then slightly unfroze as Flash roared with laughter and instantly gave Chester another loving hug. Chester let out a feeble half-laugh himself as his head was now balanced on Flash's shoulder; he didn't much like the king rat's sense of humour.

Many stories were swapped between these two leaders in the ensuing hours, and Chester was able to retell his many tales, and said that what he really wanted, above all else, was to get back home to Anfield with his new friends safe and sound.

"I can help you there," Flash boldly announced to a surprised but grateful mouse. "We will use the sewers that I know well, and as long as you stay close and do as I say, you will come to no harm. This will be the easiest part of your journey. Your troubles are at an end," and with that declaration Flash left the extremely pleased Chester speechless in his wake and with his thoughts, as he hurried off to prepare his plans.

Chester's eyes searched out Arrabella amongst the heavy throng, as the mass of bodies in all shapes and sizes danced to a beautiful tune. Many tails swished wildly, as a form of rodent hokey-cokey passed by before him. Chester could now see the object of his desires, as he noticed Bella erratically performing a bit of a tango with the clumsy-footed Mousellini. Chester tried repeatedly to force his way through the fast-moving dancing chain to reach her, but he had to abandon his endeavours and wait for a better opportunity, as on one occasion he pushed too hard to break through the rhythmic conga and was immediately trampled on. He waited and waited and then he saw his chance as there was a lull in the train, when all the rats turned to face each other and put their left legs in and their left legs out.

Chester reached Arrabella and gently tapped Mousellini on the shoulder and asked if he could take over the dance. Mousellini obliged but continued with his awkward moves. Chester stood there in amazement before bursting out laughing and telling the chef, no, it was Arrabella that he wanted to dance with. Chester and Arrabella now had the moment all to themselves. They were oblivious of all the hullabaloo and madness going on all around, as they moved closer to each other and began a very slow dance. Almost immediately their tight embrace was broken, and Chester took a step backwards as Compass tried once more to squeeze in between them.

As with all parties, this one had to come to an end. As Chester told Arrabella all about Flash's kind offer, and probably the need for an early start, every rat bade them farewell and wholeheartedly meant it, as everyone retired for the night.

The next day duly arrived and Flash gave thanks that it was a beautiful day, for if it had been raining it would have been necessary to have a delay, as flooded sewers would prove far too difficult to negotiate even for an experienced rat. Chester, Arrabella, Compass and Mousellini said goodbye to the few early risers who had come to say farewell. There were no tears, for everyone felt sure that they would meet again.

"Come on then, it's time to go. We have a long journey ahead of us, so let's make a start." The eager Flash boomed out the rallying call. The expedition was now off, led by Flash and three sizeable colleagues – just enough muscle to dissuade anyone with foolish intent along the way.

Flash entered a broken clay pipe and gestured for everyone to follow and told them not to be afraid. Chester initially showed a slight reluctance and hesitated momentarily, but then he reasoned, what could possibly go wrong in the company of all these fearsome bodyguards, but he also quickly realised that, what with his track record, it was best not to count his chickens. The old clay pipe wasn't very long – about six feet at the most. It was almost a case of up, in and out, as Flash reached the end of it in seconds and expertly dropped down onto the small algae-covered ledge below, and called back up to the tiny mice to be very careful as the narrow shelf was ever so slippery.

The nervous mice now stared in total amazement, as the full enormity of this vast cavernous world came into view. It was as if they were just minute dots, totally lost and swallowed in these huge dark and dank chambers that possessed a horrid smell all of their own. A lone but regular drip dropped from the age-old and cracked brick ceiling, exploding on entry into what appeared to be a foul-smelling stream, which trickled slowly by, just below the slippery ledge. All manner of nasty things seemed to be floating in it, but Chester didn't want to know what they were, so he didn't ask, as he closed off his nostrils until it was time to take another breath.

Flash wasted no time at all as he purposefully strode on ahead, forcing all of the mice to run and slither on the slime underfoot as they tried to keep up. Six mouse strides, it seems, were only equal to one rat stride. The odd beam of dusty light managed to intrude into the dark depths, as the world above met with the world below, and a trillion other watchful eyes could now be seen, some observing with interest and some with disdain, as the mixed troop cautiously filed by. There was nothing to worry about though, as Flash's authority and well-earned reputation would not be challenged today.

The putrid smell that hung in the air seemed to lose its intensity with every yard travelled, but this was not because it had disappeared. No, it was due more to the fact that Compass and the other mice were simply getting used to it. Suddenly Flash entered another chamber and came across what seemed to be some sort of junction, a major intersection of this sewer highway. A huge labyrinth of tunnels and interconnecting passages loomed into view, but no signposts were evident to show the way. There was no hesitation shown or uncertainty either, as Flash with his unbroken stride, chose one tunnel amongst many and disappeared within, imploring everyone to follow. They had barely been in this channel for a minute when their alert and agile leader suddenly sensed trouble and flung himself hard up against the walls, whilst impressing upon his wards the importance of quickly doing the same as a rumbling, swishing, swashing sound travelling at super speed broke the silence, drowning out the constant drips. Chester and Arrabella held hands tightly and just about managed to evade the colourful waterfall which exploded out from the small opening above. Mousellini wasn't so fortunate though as he took the full brunt of the cascading shower, which almost knocked him from his feet. The torrent subsided almost as quickly as it had come, and the drenched Italian emerged out of it coughing and spluttering and screaming abuse. Everyone ducked as he furiously shook from side to side, sending the stinky spray jetting towards them. He ranted nonstop and then ranted some more as he realised it wasn't water, but Flash reassured him that he had been very lucky and he had got off lightly, as it could have been so much worse.

The irate Mousellini, in that instant, forgot his position in the pecking order and angrily faced up to the wise Flash, demanding to know what it was he was babbling on about. Everyone once again froze, as no one had ever dared to undermine the king of rats, but Flash proved once again beyond doubt that he was a rightful leader, as he considered his reply and simply repeated his words of before: "Believe you me, it could have been much worse."

Before long, they were off again to continue with their trek, but not before Chester had apologised for his wet friend's outburst.

"Not to worry," Flash answered. "It is understandable. I would have done the same," he quietly spoke in a conciliatory tone.

## 11 Home at Last

Many miles later, and after many thoughts about whether Flash did in fact really know the way, a tremendous noise, quietly at first, began to resound all around. Their sharp ears had definitely detected it long before it gained in strength and bounced and echoed off the domed walls. Chester could now recognise the thunderous sounds, as they had arrived slowly at first, with the distant patter of footsteps that then built in intensity as they got closer and closer, like a marching army.

"It was just like my mother Maisie said!" Chester announced loudly and added excitedly, "It must be that time of the year!"

Chester, Mousellini, Arrabella, Flash and the three friendly giants all scaled the walls and thrust their heads out of the cast iron grid embedded in the gutter. Chester and Arrabella fidgeted slightly and adjusted their position as they allowed the irritating Compass to squeeze in between them. And there it was, the scene was set, just as Maisie had described in minute detail. Thousands upon thousands of screaming people had gathered. No cars could be seen, there was no space to be had as ecstatic humans cheered loudly and wildly waved multi-coloured flags. Some stuffed pastries and crisps, fish in batter, chips, and sugary sweets into welcoming mouths. Chester was totally overwhelmed as tears welled up in his eyes. His emotions were all over the place as he tearfully told Arrabella that they were now home,

"We are back in Anfield!"

Chester returned his gaze to the throng and suddenly realised his mum had got it wrong, for there wasn't one lone bus snaking its way down Oakfield Road with the masses following. No, there were two buses. One covered in red and white banners and streamers galore, and on top of it, there were humans in expensive suits holding aloft a silvery thing, but following closely behind was another coach, bedecked in the royal blue of Everton, with pennants blowing freely in the wind. It had woolen scarves hanging from its windows as another silvery thing was held high, and the sea of people, all dressed in red, white and blue, stood side by side in mutual admiration and praise, as they chanted out a loud rendition of "MERSEYSIDE, MERSEYSIDE, MERSEYSIDE."

"What a lovely day it is to return to Liverpool!" Chester thought to himself, as he felt a surge of pride run right through him. Given the fact that he had arrived home with all of his friends to witness so many happy faces and gaiety all around, Arrabella would surely be impressed, and so she was as she moved a little closer to Chester and squashed Compass.

An hour later nearly all the merriment had died down or moved on, to somewhere else. The colourful buses had long since snaked out of view, and apart from the vociferous partying at the local pub, everything returned to normal, as the fading light brought with it the most serene of moments as a peaceful lull now calmed the Anfield streets.

The four rats and the four mice had now clung to the wall under the grid for a very long time. They all decided it was time to clamber out, as their feet were now aching and their legs began to cramp, but before they could move something else moved before them, and caught the eyes of Chester first. A familiar shape he knew only too well scuttled out of the shadows, and in an instant, claimed the remnants of a pork pie all to himself.

Chester loudly exclaimed without much thought for his startled friends, who immediately stopped their clambering, "Is it …? It can't be … It is … It's *Tocky.*" Tocky, Chester's younger sibling, the mouse who liked to be first in everything he did, the one who showed imagination and a will to succeed, hadn't changed at all, as he thrust forward and greedily grabbed another part of the pie.

Almost immediately after Tocky had performed the initial risk assessment, signaling that the coast was clear, vast hordes of other mice leapt out from the shadows that had kept them hidden, and they swiftly began to gather in the plentiful bounty that now littered the vacated streets. And amidst all the tremendous kerfuffle going on before him, Chester now saw the emergence of so many familiar and friendly faces, coming out into the open. Norris, Walton, Crocky, and Belle grappled over a pepperoni pizza. Knotty and Orrell, wrestled with Faz over a sausage roll as Dingle looked on. Gatty reduced Gil – ah! little Gil – to tears as he pinched a bourbon biscuit from under her nose, and Dove nibbled at a bun that nobody else wanted. Club and Edge though were involved in a mighty tussle as a tug-of-war developed between them on one end of a doner kebab and a huge stranger holding on tightly at the other end. Chester suddenly recognised who the stranger was, and wondered how on earth Mousellini had managed to get out of the grid without being spotted. Eventually though, Club and Edge relented and gave up the prize, as a powerful nasty smell, one which they had never experienced before, attacked their sensitive nostrils.

The joy Chester was feeling as he jumped out and above, dragging Arrabella with him, knew no bounds. He thought it couldn't get any better, but it did, as, wandering into view with a more leisurely approach which said, "I've seen it and done it all before," was Chester's loving mum, Maisie, closely followed by Handsome Ted, and he was followed even more closely by seven infant mice. There was a great coming together in the next few moments, as Chester made his entrance and took his close-knit family by surprise. Hugs, tears, cuddles, you name it, they were all there. Emotions were running very high as everyone re-acquainted themselves with each other. Lots of introductions ensued, but it took a little while for Flash and his friends to be accepted. But eventually they were, as nervous mice who had bolted for cover re-emerged and made the rats most welcome.

A party to end all parties would take place that night, as Flash sent word for his many friends to come and join in the fun. Maisie had all her family around her once more, and lots of friends and other relatives made their way over from Goodison Park, Everton, to join in the festivities. Dancing and frivolity, music and laughter, were the order of the day, as the mega-party lasted long into the night. The only sour note that occurred though was when Maisie slapped Handsome Ted's face as he moved closer and gave her that familiar wink.

A few months later, Chester and Arrabella were married under the floorboards of the now centrally heated Victorian terrace house in St. Domingo Vale, Anfield. Thousands of mice were in attendance, and many had travelled from near and far, for the legend of Chester was now deeply engrained in mouse folklore.

A daft mouse from Liverpool, who many thought never stood a chance, had overcome the many doubters and even more obstacles. He had scaled dizzy heights few others could ever have achieved, and he had brought the mouse and rat communities together, who now worked in harmony as they raided food stores all over the world, for news travelled fast. Everyone helped each other and helped some more, as a newly acquired togetherness flourished and grew. Chester took a bite out of the wedding breakfast of moussaka, lovingly prepared by Mousellini's hand. Chester had asked for very little cheese, but as always, the Italian chef hadn't listened.

As the day wore on and the festivities continued, Chester returned to his room and slumped down onto his comfy bed. He began to reflect once more about everything and anything and everyone as warm tears swamped his eyes and then overflowed, rolling gently down his cheeks. He could see in his mind Peregrine soaring high, gracefully performing acrobatics in a beautiful sky. He thought about the many friends he had and the ones he had lost. He thought about Arrabella, now his wife, Maisie his mum, the old lady who called out to him with that familiar cry, "And how are you today little Mousie?" and so much more, until he just rolled over, and buried his head deep into his pillow and cried uncontrollably, and the soft covering of paper and straw swelled as it absorbed the salty liquid. Arrabella had quietly entered the room, and watched from a distance the sorrowful sobbing from her new husband. She slowly approached a few moments later and sat down to comfort the mouse she loved. She didn't ask Chester the reason for his upset, but it quickly became apparent as he wiped his eyes and asked, "Do you know, if we have children, can we call our first son GIBLET?"

The End

Printed in Great Britain
by Amazon

32790363R00118